A READER'S GUIDE TO

R.A. SALVATORE'S

THE LEGEND OF DRIZZT

A READER'S GUIDE TO

R.A. SALVATORE'S

THE LEGEND OF
DRIZZT

A READER'S GUIDE TO
R.A. SALVATORE'S
THE LEGEND OF DRIZZT

©2008 Wizards of the Coast, Inc.

Published by Wizards of the Coast, Inc. FORGOTTEN REALMS, THE LEGEND OF DRIZZT,
WIZARDS OF THE COAST, and their respective logos are trademarks of Wizards of the
Coast, Inc., in the U.S.A. and other countries.

Printed in the U.S.A.

First Printing: August 2008

9 8 7 6 5 4 3 2 1

ISBN: 978-0-7869-4915-1
620-21816720-001-EN

Library of Congress Cataloging-in-Publication Data:

Athans, Philip.
A reader's guide to R.A. Salvatore's The legend of Drizzt / Philip Athans.
    p. cm.
ISBN 978-0-7869-4915-1
1. Salvatore, R. A., 1959- Legend of Drizzt--Handbooks, manuals, etc.
2. Drizzt Do'Urden (Fictitious character)--Handbooks, manuals, etc. I. Title.
  PS3569.A462345Z53 2008
  813'.54--dc22

                                                                2008021452

U.S., CANADA, ASIA, PACIFIC,   EUROPEAN HEADQUARTERS
& LATIN AMERICA   Hasbro UK Ltd
Wizards of the Coast, Inc.   Caswell Way
P.O. Box 707   Newport, Gwent NP9 0YH
Renton, WA 98057-0707   GREAT BRITAIN
+1-800-324-6496   Save this address for your records.

Visit our web site at
www.wizards.com

Text by Philip Athans
Edited by Susan J. Morris
Art Direction by Matt Adelsperger
Designed by Dan Colavito
Cover Art by Todd Lockwood

Researchers: Douglas N. Burke,
Jay Cox, Tim Haney,
Jeremy Henn, John Maniha,
Christina Rowe, George Mears,
Eric Noah, James Ross,
and Sandra Salla.

CONTENTS

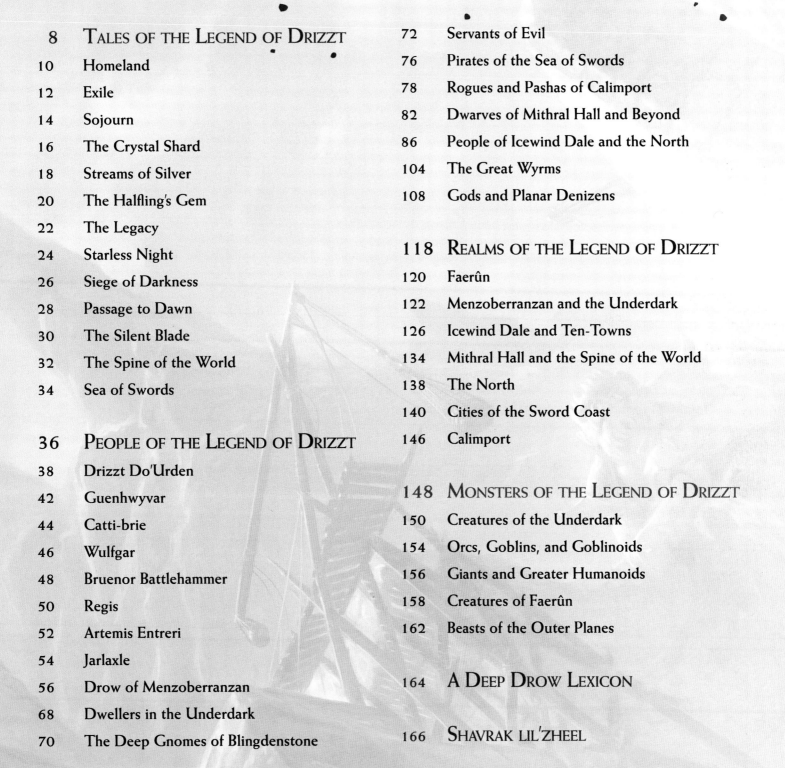

Featured Artist: Todd Lockwood
Cartography: Adam Gillespie, Robert Lazzaretti, and Todd Gamble
Interior Artists: Tom Baxa, Carl Critchlow, Wayne England, Lucio Parillo, Kieran Yanner, Beth Trott, and Francis Tsai, Daren Bader, Beet, Steve Belledin, Brom, Matt Cavotta, Mitch Cotie, Ed Cox, Eric Deschamps, Brian Despain, Michael Dutton, Jeff Easley, Steve Ellis, Larry Elmore, Mark Evans, Emily Fiegenschuh, Fred Fields, Jon Foster, Carl Frank, Randy Gallegos, Lars Grant-West, David Griffith, Rebecca Guay, Brian Hagan, Fred Hooper, David Hudnut, Heather Hudson, Jackoilrain, Vince Locke, Howard Lyon, Roberto Marchesi, Matthew Mitchell, Raven Mimura, Christopher Moeller, Duane O. Myers, Jim Nelson, William O'Connor, Keith Parkinson, Jim Pavelec, Michael Phillipi, Alan Pollack, Steve Prescott, Adam Rex, Wayne Reynolds, Robh Ruppel, Richard Sardinha, Mike Sass, Marc Sasso, Dan Scott, Ron Spencer, Matthew Stawicki, Matthew Stewart, Justin Sweet, Arnie Swekel, Stephen Tappin, Joel Thomas, Franz Vohwinkel, Kev Walker, Eva Widermann, Matt Wilson, Sam Wood, and James Zhang

FOREWORD
BY R.A. SALVATORE

I guess you know you've really made it when they do a coffee table retrospective on your work, eh? (Stop snickering—my mom is Canadian!)

I've never been big on dates, or time, or even what day of the week it happens to be, and of course all of that is reinforced by the fact that I've been at a job for most of my adult life where Saturday is no different than Monday is no different than Wednesday, except that there are better shows on the History and Discovery channels on Saturday. Because of simple survival instinct, I do remember the birthdays of those close, and of course my anniversary, but the numbers associated with (constraining, even) time have always seemed somewhat of an arbitrary thing to me.

Having said all of that, the notion that this is the twentieth anniversary of the Drizzt books has settled on my shoulders rather profoundly, and has forced me to take a long and wistful look at this incredible journey I've been so fortunate to experience. I look back now across the decades, at all the people whom I've met and worked with, at all the fans with whom I've interacted (so many, many more now that we have witnessed such a dramatic change in the very nature of human interaction). It stuns me to look back on how different the world was when I started the Drizzt books almost as much as it shocks me to realize that Drizzt is older than many of my readers! Think about that; this character got jumped by yetis in Icewind Dale before many of the people reading this introduction and the retrospective were even born.

Dang, I feel old!

So when I look back at "Drizzt," it's really not about Drizzt at all, but about the road we've walked together. It took me to my first airplane ride, to Gen Con in Milwaukee in 1989, and on more than a hundred similar trips since. This road has led me to Lake Geneva, Wisconsin and to Renton, Washington. It led me to New York, where I did my first non-FORGOTTEN REALMS® novels and to Skywalker Ranch to work with George Lucas and his amazing team on a couple of STAR WARS® books. Because of Drizzt, I got to write a story about Luke Skywalker . . . I mean, wow! This road has taken me to England and Italy, to San Diego Comic-Con and Indianapolis. It led me to Florida and a small comic publisher named CrossGen, and that brought me to a wonderful relationship that continues to this day with the good folks at Devil's Due. Because of Drizzt, a young Pennsylvania high school kid named Joe sent me a letter, and kept my reply, and when the internet started booming, he quickly secured the URL www.rasalvatore.com. He offered it to me for free if only I would look at his web site, and I was so impressed and so touched that I told him to keep the URL; that web site is running smoothly and has a fantastic group of folks I've come to know as friends.

Because of Drizzt, a Boston Red Sox pitcher called me up and asked me to come and join his video game team—and I got to go to Fenway to watch World Series games. How cool is that?

And most of all, because of this road, I've had the distinct privilege to be invited into the thoughts of so many people, and the opportunity to touch their lives in whatever small manner. Maybe my Drizzt stories have helped turn someone on to reading, or helped someone get through a particularly dark time, or maybe these books have just given someone something to grumble and complain about! In any case, it's been an amazing and wonderful journey.

One of my good fortunes along this road has been my association with Phil Athans. Phil became my editor when I rejoined the FORGOTTEN REALMS team after Wizards of the Coast bought out TSR. He came recommended by Mary Kirchoff, who had resumed duties as the manager of the team (and who, of course, had been the one to fish me out of a slush pile back in 1987, and who remains a dear, dear friend to this day!). It didn't take Phil and me long to get past the editor-author relationship and to become good friends. He "gets" what I do, and understands as well as anyone I've ever met the difficulties of writing novels in a shared world, a shared game setting, a shared environment. He knows the writing process from both sides, having penned many books himself, including *Annihilation*, which I consider one of the high points of the War of the Spider Queen series based upon my work with

the drow of Menzoberranzan (and also a heck of a lot of fun, as I got to edit Phil on that one . . . but that's another story).

When Wizards first approached me about doing this Reader's Guide, the first question I asked was, "Who's writing it?" I already knew the answer; there could have been only one answer. There is only one person who understands the dramatic changes that have come over the Realms in the last decade and at the same time recognizes the way I've tried to incorporate or simply stay out of the way of those changes.

There is no one other than Phil who could have properly pulled all of this information together into this format, and few others I would have trusted with the project. Phil knows the Realms as well as anyone alive, and knows my place in it. He takes care of Drizzt as he takes care of me. He's a friend to us both.

So thanks, Phil, for making your schedule just a little bit crazier to help us all take a good long look at who Drizzt is and where he came from, and how we all got to this incredible place.

Peace,

R.A. Salvatore

TALES OF THE LEGEND OF DRIZZT

As soon as he landed, two dark elves burst out of doors set in the back of the balcony, against the mound. A silver-streaking arrow greeted the first, blowing her back into the carved room, and Entreri made short work of the other, finishing her before Drizzt and Catti-brie had even leaped across to join him. Then came Guenhwyvar, the panther flying past the three surprised companions to take up the lead along the stairway.

—*Starless Night*

THE LEGEND OF DRIZZT BOOK I
HOMELAND

Drizzt looked out into the myriad colors and shapes that composed Menzoberranzan. "What is this place?" he whispered, realizing how little he knew of his homeland beyond the walls of his own house. Zak's words—Zak's rage—pressed in on Drizzt as he stood there, reminding him of his ignorance and hinting at a dark path ahead.

In the subterranean city of Menzoberranzan, the drow clan House Do'Urden, led by Matron Malice, prepares for war against rival House Devir. Dinin Do'Urden, one of Matron Malice's wicked sons, hires the Faceless One, a powerful and mysterious wizard, to aid their efforts while the priestesses of Lolth prepare for the imminent birth of Malice's sixth child.

The attack on House Devir is launched at the same time Malice gives birth to Drizzt Do'Urden—one too many boys for the matriarchal noble House. Zaknafein, the weapons master of House Do'Urden and Drizzt's father, leads the wholesale slaughter of House Devir. In the thick of battle, Dinin kills his older brother Nalfein, which causes the priestesses to halt the ritual that would have ended with the sacrifice of the infant Drizzt.

The Faceless One fails to assassinate Alton Devir, who is saved when one of the Faceless One's own apprentices, Masoj Hun'ett, turns on his master. Alton vows to take revenge on House Do'Urden in the guise of the Faceless One.

Drizzt grows up under the watchful eye of his sister Vierna. Their mother intends for Drizzt to become a wizard, but Zaknafein sees more potential in the young drow's skill at arms. The weapons master begins to train Drizzt himself, nurturing both his son's swordsmanship and his burgeoning conscience—a trait so rare among drow that it's nearly unheard of.

Eventually Malice sends Drizzt to finish his training at Melee-Magthere, where he continues to grow as a swordsman. In his final year of study, Drizzt attends lessons in magic with Masoj and meets the disguised Alton Devir, and Masoj's panther, Guenhwyvar.

After serving on a patrol in which he spares the life of Ellifain, a surface elf child, and briefly befriends the deep gnome Belwar Dissengulp, Drizzt returns to House Do'Urden and reunites with Zaknafein. Malice finally becomes fully aware of how different her son and his father are, and recognizes the danger their feelings represent to the matriarchy. Zaknafein realizes that Malice has finally decided to kill his son, and offers his own life in exchange for Drizzt's. Malice accepts.

Drizzt, who has fled into the Underdark alone, battles for his life against a cave fisher. Guenhwyvar, who is about to kill Drizzt at Masoj's command, helps Drizzt instead, choosing to side with Drizzt against both Masoj and Alton.

Finally Drizzt returns home, only to find that Zaknafein is dead. Drizzt formally denounces Lolth, his mother, and his House and escapes, alone once again, into the Underdark.

1 HOUSE FAEN-TLABBAR

The faerie fire that decorates the eastern towers of House Faen-Tlabbar reveals the spider theme common among the Lolth-worshiping Houses of Menzoberranzan. Led by Matron Mother Ghenni'tiroth Tlabbar, the priestesses of the Fourth House are particularly cruel, fanatically devout servants of the Queen of the Demonweb Pits. Like the other noble Houses of the City of Spiders, Faen-Tlabbar maintains a complex of hundreds of rooms carved into enormous stalagmites rising out of the cavern floor.

2 THE VIEW FROM QU'ELLARZ'ORL

Drizzt and Guenhwyvar stand on the far western end of the high shelf of Qu'ellarz'orl, overlooking the Narbondellyn district. A great forest of giant mushrooms stretches off to the east, and Houses Mizzrym and Agrach Dyrr are not far away. The Chamber of the Ruling Council is just in front of them. The only light comes from the faerie fire-adorned towers, the drow in the streets disappearing into the ever-present darkness of the City of Spiders.

3 GIANT MUSHROOMS

Countless varieties of mushrooms are found in Menzoberranzan. Most of the furniture in any given drow city will be crafted out of their lightweight but sturdy wood, and along with the meat of the cattlelike rothé, the mushroom is a vital food staple. Special varieties of mushrooms are also grown as ingredients for potions and poisons. The mushroom groves are tended by orc and goblin slaves.

THE LEGEND OF DRIZZT BOOK II
EXILE

Clacker looked all around, and then up. Other mind flayers were drifting down from the ceiling, two holding Drizzt by the ankles. More invisible doors opened. In an instant, blast after blast came at Clacker from every angle, and the defense of his dual personalities' inner turmoil quickly began to wear away. Desperation and welling outrage took over Clacker's actions.

Drizzt Do'Urden has left Menzoberranzan, the cruel city of his birth, far behind. Still winding his way through the perilous Underdark, he struggles with a loneliness that threatens to crush even his seemingly indomitable will.

At the same time, back in the City of Spiders, Matron Mother Malice is rescued from certain death by House Baenre. She is told that the spider goddess Lolth demands that her renegade son be sacrificed—a sacrifice Malice is all too happy to make.

Drizzt travels to the svirfneblin city of Blingdenstone, where he once again encounters Belwar, the deep gnome he saved many years before. The deep gnomes allow Drizzt to stay in their city until rumors and signs make it clear that a powerful creature is hunting the renegade dark elf. This creature is Zaknafein, Drizzt's father, whom Malice has returned from the dead in the form of a spirit-wraith under her control.

Drizzt and Belwar abandon Blingdenstone to carve out a living in the Underdark, but are pursued by the undead Zaknafein. They meet and befriend Clacker, a pech—one of a race of small humanoids that calls the Underdark home—who has been transformed by a mad wizard into a terrible monster called a hook horror. The three are soon captured by a community of illithids.

Zaknafein can't stop his relentless search for his son, and he soon finds Drizzt, now a slave to the dreaded mind flayers. The undead drow weapons master causes enough chaos in the illithid caverns that Drizzt, Belwar, and Clacker are able to flee. All the while, Zaknafein struggles to overcome Malice's domination of his will.

Still under an uncontrollable compulsion, Zaknafein tracks them down once more, and this time it's Clacker who pays the ultimate price. The weapons master continues to resist the compulsion to serve, and during a brief moment of clarity, Zaknafein is finally able to overcome Malice's control of his spirit, but only long enough to save his son by sacrificing himself. Zaknafein throws his undead body into a lake of acid, and Drizzt is free to escape into the Underdark once more.

Malice's failure dooms her, and all Menzoberranzan rises up against House Do'Urden.

Drizzt realizes that as long as he remains in the Underdark, he'll never get far enough away from the fanatical hatred of the City of Spiders and its arachnid goddess. He leaves Belwar in Blingdenstone and sets out for the vast, unknown reaches of the World Above.

1   SPIRIT-WRAITH

Created by a ritual granted by the Spider Queen to only her most favored priestesses, the *zin-carla* (translated from Undercommon as "spirit-wraith") is the animated corpse of a recently dead drow. The deceased's soul is dragged from the afterlife and returned to its body, its will subject to the commands of the priestess who completes the ritual. A spirit-wraith retains the memory of its past life, but suffers in thrall to its new mistress. Sometimes a *zin-carla* is able to overpower the compulsion to serve, and when it does, it seeks its revenge against the priestess who created it.

2   ILLITHIDS

The dreaded mind flayers, illithids are creatures of horrifying evil. Possessed of powerful psionic abilities, they hunger for the thoughts, memories, emotions, ideas, and even the very brains of any sentient being unfortunate enough to encounter them. Though roughly humanoid in form, that is where any similarity to humans ends. The tentacles that dominate their faces bore into their victims' heads, seeking out their brains, and the horrific feast begins. Though they're occasionally found in tenuous alliance with dark elves and other beings, they care nothing for concepts like relationships and politics.

THE LEGEND OF DRIZZT BOOK III
SOJOURN

"How would a dark elf know of a bear?" Montolio asked aloud, still scratching at his beard. The ranger considered two possibilities: Either there was more to the drow race than he knew, or this particular dark elf was not akin to his kin.

The renegade dark elf Drizzt Do'Urden has come to the World Above, with Guenhwyvar at his side. He encounters a tribe of gnolls and reluctantly travels with them but turns on the vicious creatures when they prepare to ambush a family of humans. Drizzt dispatches the gnolls and saves the Thistledown family from certain death.

Even then, the suspicious humans are terrified of this lone drow, believing him to be even more dangerous than the gnolls. What's worse, the gnolls he killed served the barghests Ulgulu and Kempfana, who vow to kill the one responsible for their servants' destruction.

Word spreads of this curious dark elf, and Roddy McGristle is hired to track him down. McGristle is scarred in his first engagement with Drizzt, and one of his loyal hounds is killed. This only serves to anger the human, who vows revenge.

Ulgulu finds and slaughters the Thistledowns, leaving a scimitar at the scene in an effort to implicate Drizzt, who finds the bodies and flees.

Dove Falconhand, one of the fabled Seven Sisters, steps in to help find this murderous drow, and McGristle also remains hot on his trail. Drizzt captures Tephanis, the barghests' quickling spy, who tells him of the barghests. With Guenhwyvar's help, Drizzt tracks down Ulgulu and Kempfana and kills them.

Dove and McGristle eventually join forces, and as they track Drizzt, they discover clues to indicate that the dark elf is innocent of the murders. When they finally find him, Drizzt ends up helping them fend off an attack by stone giants, and all but Roddy McGristle are inclined to believe in Drizzt's innocence.

Drizzt finds his way to a valley that is the home of the blind ranger Montolio deBrouchee. Montolio takes Drizzt under his wing, teaching him the secrets of the ranger and the ways of the goddess Mielikki.

Roddy McGristle, still on Drizzt's trail, can't find the hidden valley until Tephanis leads him to it. McGristle and Tephanis ally with the orc chieftain Graul and attack the valley—but are driven back by Drizzt and Montolio.

Drizzt stays with Montolio for a time, but when the ranger dies, Drizzt leaves the grove. He encounters a strange group called the Weeping Friars, whom he helps sneak past the red dragon Hephaestus, then he heads for the remote human settlements of Ten-Towns. There, Drizzt settles down in the harsh tundra and meets Catti-brie and her dwarf "father," Bruenor Battlehammer. Roddy McGristle tracks him there but is again chased off by Drizzt. The lone dark elf decides to stay on in the frozen tundra of Icewind Dale.

1 BLUSTER

Drizzt first encounters the great brown bear Bluster in a cave, where the animal is hibernating. Though the fierce predator is easily riled and has a growl like an avalanche, Drizzt befriends him by giving him food, and somehow Bluster senses that Drizzt and Guenhwyvar are not his enemies. It is this relationship with the great bear that impresses the ranger Montolio enough to even consider taking a strange dark elf under his wing.

2 HOOTER

Likely the first owl—maybe the first bird of prey—that Drizzt encounters upon emerging from the Underdark onto the World Above, Hooter is a close companion of the blind ranger Montolio and acts as his scout. When Hooter requires Montolio's attention, he rings a silver bell.

3 TEPHANIS

Tephanis is a quickling, which is a fey creature related to the brownie; but in the distant past, the quicklings embraced a malign form of magic and became the dark beings they are today. Lethal despite their tiny stature, quicklings are essentially invisible when they stand still, which thankfully isn't often. Tephanis speaks so quickly that to a human ear it sounds like nothing more than an irritating buzzing noise. The cocky Tephanis is also skilled at picking locks and spends his short life (quicklings die of old age by thirteen) causing nothing but trouble.

THE LEGEND OF DRIZZT BOOK IV
THE CRYSTAL SHARD

The liches, undead spirits of powerful wizards that refused to rest when their mortal bodies had passed from the realms of the living, had gathered to create the most vile artifact ever made, an evil that fed and flourished off of that which the purveyors of good considered most precious— the light of the sun.

Akar Kessell, an apprentice mage, is stranded in Icewind Dale, where he happens upon Crenshinibon. The ancient artifact, also known simply as the Crystal Shard, twists Kessell's desperate mind and rewards him with wizardly power beyond his meager training. The relic raises a great crystal tower, Cryshal-Tirith, to serve as Kessell's stronghold.

Meanwhile, the barbarian tribes of Icewind Dale unite against the people of Ten-Towns. Drizzt, Regis, and Bruenor rush to warn the townsfolk. They succeed in repelling the barbarians, who are all but wiped out. One of the few survivors is Wulfgar, captured in battle by Bruenor. The dwarf takes in the young barbarian, demanding five years of service.

Nearly five years pass while Wulfgar labors in the dwarven mines. He and Bruenor have developed a bond based on mutual respect. When Bruenor fashions the mighty enchanted warhammer, Aegis-fang, he gives it to Wulfgar to wield.

Akar Kessell builds an army of humanoids, with powerful allies like the barbarian king Heafstaag, the frost giant Biggrin, and even the great balor Errtu, who came to Faerûn on the trail of Crenshinibon.

Drizzt and his companions learn of Akar Kessell and his plans to enslave Ten-Towns. Once more they attempt to unite the townsfolk against a common enemy but this time with less success.

While the folk of Ten-Towns do nothing to prepare for the coming onslaught, the newly freed Wulfgar goes out in search of the white dragon Icingdeath. With the help of Drizzt, the great wyrm is destroyed, and Drizzt claims from its horde the enchanted scimitar that will forever bear the dragon's name.

Wulfgar challenges Heafstaag and defeats him. Using the dragon's treasure as payment, Wulfgar gathers Heafstaag's tribe to march to Ten-Towns—but this time, the barbarians aim to *defend* the towns.

The overly confident Kessell orders his attack and raises a third crystal tower near the town of Bryn Shander, further draining the extraordinary, but not limitless, power of Crenshinibon. While Bryn Shander is under siege by the humanoids, giants, and barbarian tribes under Kessell's control, Drizzt battles Errtu, and with the help of the enchanted scimitar Icingdeath, the dark elf wins the day.

By blocking the sunlight it needs to fuel its magic, Drizzt further weakens the Crystal Shard and manages to tear down the third Cryshal-Tirith. Stinging from its defeat, Crenshinibon blames the inexperienced Akar Kessell, and the upstart wizard is buried with the Crystal Shard under an avalanche.

Aided by Wulfgar's barbarian mercenaries, Ten-Towns drives back the rest of Kessell's horde. Ten-Towns is once again safe, and Drizzt, Regis, and Bruenor, now joined by Wulfgar, leave Icewind Dale on a mission to find the dwarf's lost home, Mithral Hall.

1 CRYSHAL-TIRITH

These enormous towers of sparkling crystal are raised by Crenshinibon at the request of Akar Kessell. From within, Kessell is able to scry his enemies and is protected by the Crystal Shard's extraordinary magic. The Cryshal-Tirith reacts to the evil whims of its "master" in seemingly limitless ways, even emitting a searing ray of heat to blast unsuspecting enemies. The tower itself appears as a duplicate of the Crystal Shard, but thousands of times its size.

2 VERBEEGS

The so-called "human behemoths" dwell throughout the windswept expanse of Icewind Dale and are often found acting as leaders to less intelligent giantkin like ogres and hill giants. At up to ten feet tall, they cut an imposing figure striding through the snowfields armed with primitive but deadly weapons and wrapped in skins (human skins, as often as not) and furs. Verbeegs tend to suffer from one physical deformity or another, which can fool an enemy into thinking of them as nothing but brutes, but they're as intelligent as any human and driven by selfish cunning.

THE LEGEND OF DRIZZT BOOK V
STREAMS OF SILVER

Wulfgar moved the torch closer to the gap and they all saw clearly the curving arc that could only be the wood of a longbow, and the silvery shine of a bowstring. Wulfgar grasped the wood and tugged lightly, expecting it to break apart in his hands under the enormous weight of the stone.

Drizzt, Regis, and Wulfgar, led by Bruenor, leave Icewind Dale in search of Mithral Hall, the fabled home of Clan Battlehammer. Behind them in Ten-Towns, the assassin Artemis Entreri has come in search of Regis but finds Catti-brie instead, terrifying her before he disappears.

In the port city of Luskan, Bruenor acquires a map to help them find Mithral Hall. At the Hosttower of the Arcane, home of the wizards who secretly rule Luskan, Dendybar the Mottled and his lieutenants, Sydney and Jierdan, look on as Drizzt and company leave the city. Believing Drizzt to be in possession of the Crystal Shard, they summon the spirit of Morkai the Red to discover what has brought Drizzt and his friends to Luskan.

Catti-brie sets out to find her friends but once again falls into the clutches of Entreri, and both of them are summoned to the Hosttower. The wizards offer to "help," and Entreri, Jierdan, Sydney, and the flesh golem Bok leave Luskan in search of the companions, with Catti-brie as their prisoner.

Drizzt and his friends are beset by orcs and barbarians, then are turned away from the town of Nesmé to fight their way through the dangerous Evermoors only to be turned away from the gates of Silverymoon. But Alustriel, the city's leader and one of the Seven Sisters, visits Drizzt and advises him to seek out the Herald's Holdfast. There they learn the probable location of Mithral Hall.

Catti-brie escapes from her captors, and she's reunited with her friends at the doorway to Mithral Hall. Entering the hall, Bruenor recovers the armor and crown of his ancestors and proclaims himself the Eighth King of Mithral Hall. The companions explore as far as Garumn's Gorge and discover that the furnaces are still afire.

Dendybar once again summons Morkai and learns the location of Mithral Hall. Sydney and Entreri pursue their quarry there, and Bok breaks down the door. They eventually find Drizzt and his companions, and Entreri and the dark elf face off. It appears that both are killed.

Bruenor, Wulfgar, Regis, and Catti-brie battle duergar and retrieve the fabled bow Taulmaril. Drizzt and Entreri, lost deep within Mithral Hall, battle their way back to the companions, together cutting down and tricking duergar patrols along the way.

The battle is joined at Garumn's Gorge where Bruenor concentrates on defeating the shadow dragon Shimmergloom. He is assumed lost in the effort, while Entreri succeeds in capturing Regis, and Sydney tries once again to recover the Crystal Shard. Barely escaping with their lives, Catti-brie, Drizzt, and Wulfgar regroup at the Ivy Mansion, where Catti-brie decides to raise and lead an army back to Mithral Hall, and Drizzt and Wulfgar prepare to rescue Regis from the assassin. Dendybar falls to the evil Morkai, and something stirs at the bottom of Garumn's Gorge.

1 CLAN BATTLEHAMMER

This clan of sturdy dwarves once lived hundreds of miles from their current home in Icewind Dale, where they occupy a valley north of Bryn Shander near Kelvin's Cairn. They're led by Bruenor Battlehammer, a direct descendant of Gandalug Battlehammer, the First King of Mithral Hall. Dwarf clans are close-knit societies: part tribe, part merchant company, and part extended family. These battle-hardened warriors work their mines in Icewind Dale but always dream of returning to their glorious roots in the subterranean city of Mithral Hall.

2 DUERGAR

Also known as gray dwarves, the duergar inhabit the upper reaches of the Underdark. They're as hardworking as their surface kin but follow a darker path and a darker god. Their cities, which they guard with fanatical zeal, are as corrupt and violent as any drow enclave, and as a race they're almost as dangerous as the drow. Duergar have an innate ability to render themselves invisible, making them accomplished sneak thieves and ambushers. They trade with the drow when they aren't fighting against them.

BOK, THE FLESH GOLEM

Flesh golems are horrific constructs made from pieces of human corpses sewn together and brought to "life" by arcane magic. Eight feet tall and endowed with superhuman strength, Bok, like others of his kind, has little if any consciousness of his own and is fully in thrall to the wizard who created him. Flesh golems are prone to sudden and violent rages, almost as though they're momentarily aware of their grotesque, unnatural state and are driven berserk by their outrage.

THE LEGEND OF DRIZZT BOOK VI
THE HALFLING'S GEM

The assassin, mesmerized, watched as the ruby turned slowly in the candlelight. No jeweler had cut it; its precision went beyond a level attainable with an instrument. This was an artifact of magic, a creation designed, he reminded himself cautiously, to pull a viewer into that descending swirl, into the serenity of the reddened depths of the stone.

Regis has been captured by the assassin Artemis Entreri, who is taking him south to Calimport. There, Pasha Pook, leader of a dangerous thieves' guild, waits to punish Regis for stealing his enchanted ruby pendant. But Drizzt and Wulfgar are hot on their trail.

And Entreri would like nothing more than to be found. He's determined to once again face off against Drizzt, to demonstrate to the dark elf that fighting skill can only come at the cost of emotions like love. Drizzt is eager to prove him wrong. Questioning Entreri's resolve, Pook hires the pirate Pinochet to waylay *Sea Sprite*, the ship on which Drizzt and Wulfgar are traveling south.

Catti-brie has remained in Ten-Towns to raise an army to retake Mithral Hall and avenge the supposed death of the heroic Bruenor. As she gathers forces from Clan Battlehammer, from the barbarians of Icewind Dale, and from the dwarves of Citadel Adbar, she's unaware that Bruenor survived his battle with the shadow dragon Shimmergloom.

While Catti-brie's army prepares to reclaim the hall, Alustriel, one of the Chosen of Mystra, brings Catti-brie and Bruenor together, restores the dwarf king's health, and reunites them with Drizzt and Wulfgar aboard *Sea Sprite*— just as Pinochet attacks. *Sea Sprite*'s valiant crew, aided by the reunited Companions of the Hall, captures Pinochet.

Sea Sprite is damaged, though, and must put into Memnon for repairs, forcing the companions to travel overland to Calimport. Regis has been delivered to Pasha Pook and is already suffering the master thief's tortures.

In the sprawling, crowded city of Calimport, the companions search for their friend and find their way down into the sewers, where Drizzt once again faces off against Entreri. Drizzt gains the upper hand and escapes.

After fighting their way into the guild, but before they can reach Regis, the friends are confronted by Pook's wizard, LaValle, who uses the Taros Hoop to consign them to the hellish dimension of Tarterus. Regis manages to wrest the Taros Hoop's trigger from LaValle and follows his friends into Tarterus. They have to fight their way out, but thanks to Regis, they have the means to return to the Prime Material Plane.

With the aid of Guenhwyvar and a pride of Astral cats, Drizzt and his friends defeat Pasha Pook, and Regis assumes control of the guild. Leaving the halfling in his new post, the others head back north.

The time has come for Bruenor to lead Catti-brie's assembled armies to the gates of Mithral Hall.

1 DEMODANDS

Native to the dark plane of Tarterus, demodands are intelligent, cruel, and malicious beings. They've carved out petty baronies across the expanse of their home plane, a place they leave only rarely and reluctantly. They are occasionally summoned by dark mages and even darker priests to serve as guardians, or worse, as executioners.

2 TARTERUS

Great bridges of jagged stone crisscross the sunless plane of Tarterus. Seemingly devoid of land masses, these bridges are the only solid footing found in what is otherwise an endless expanse of smoke and darkness. Stomach-churning odors and cries of inhuman anguish fill air so thick and oppressive that it's hard even to walk through it. This is a place of pure evil, where no good can prosper, and creatures out of nightmares reign.

THE TAROS HOOP

The Taros Hoop is an artifact that can be used to scry distant locations or to travel to other planes. Tall enough for a man to walk through, it's mounted on a rolling frame that keeps it a foot off the floor. Within it is a weblike network of interwoven strands. When activated by a scepter capped with a huge black pearl, sparks of lightning play over the strands and coalesce into a blue glow. With the proper incantation, the hoop can be tuned to a specific place, and anyone stepping through is transported there—even if "there" is across the endless multiverse itself.

THE LEGEND OF DRIZZT BOOK VII
THE LEGACY

Vierna had exacted the ultimate punishment of drow society on troublesome Dinin, something only a high priestess in the highest favor of Lolth could ever accomplish. She had replaced Dinin's graceful drow body with this grotesque and mutated arachnid form, had replaced Dinin's fierce independence with a malevolent demeanor that she could bend to her every whim.

Drizzt's sister Vierna Do'Urden, his brother Dinin, and the mercenary leader Jarlaxle Baenre plot against Drizzt. Vierna has sent a mysterious human spy to find him.

In Mithral Hall, Catti-brie intends to marry Wulfgar. Drizzt is torn by his own emerging feelings for Catti-brie but keeps his peace. Regis has returned from Calimport, ostensibly for the wedding. But the wedding plans are put on hold when goblins begin to make their presence known in the deep tunnels under Mithral Hall.

While Drizzt and Wulfgar fight over Catti-brie, Bruenor leads an expedition into the deep tunnels and fights goblins and their ettin comrades. Thanks to a complex device that Bruenor calls "the juicer," the dwarves beat back the goblin incursion.

Vierna, feeling that Drizzt is close, performs a divine ritual to turn her brother Dinin into a hideous half-drow, half-spider creature called a drider.

When dwarves come up missing, Drizzt investigates and realizes that the dwarves were killed by drow. At the same time, Thibbledorf Pwent, lost two hundred years ago while fighting Shimmergloom, reappears after searching far and wide for lost Clan Battlehammer.

Regis and Drizzt are attacked by drow, and it's revealed that Regis isn't Regis but Artemis Entreri in disguise. Drizzt is captured by drow and dragged off on a caravan bound for Menzoberranzan. Entreri travels with the drow—he's fostering an alliance between his thieves' guild in Calimport and Jarlaxle's Bregan D'aerthe.

While the forces of Mithral Hall gather against the drow threat, Drizzt and Entreri duel, and Drizzt escapes. Down in the Underdark, he finds the real Regis, a captive of Entreri.

Drizzt and Entreri face off again, but their fight is broken up by drow. Eventually Drizzt and Entreri team up against the dark elves and defeat them, but then Entreri escapes.

In the battle against the drow, Wulfgar and Catti-brie encounter a yochlol that was summoned by Vierna. In a heroic effort to save Catti-brie from the demon, Wulfgar sacrifices himself and is killed, buried under tons of falling stone. His body is never recovered.

Drizzt and Entreri cross blades again on the surface, and Entreri barely escapes by flying from a cliff with the aid of a magic item.

A pitched battle between the dwarves of Mithral Hall and Vierna's drow ensues in which Drizzt eventually duels Vierna and kills her, Bruenor kills the drider Dinin, and Jarlaxle—always looking out for himself—escapes.

Regis finds Entreri hanging from a mountain spur. The assassin has survived, but is terribly wounded. In Mithral Hall, there's little feeling of celebration, only mourning for the fallen Wulfgar.

In the end, Matron Baenre's true plan is revealed. Ultimately she intends to conquer Mithral Hall with the aid of the spirit of Gandalug Battlehammer, the First King of Mithral Hall, whom she captured two thousand years ago.

DROW POISON

A thick, black semiliquid into which dark elves dip the tips of their crossbow bolts, the poison induces a deep sleep in its victim that can last as long as eight hours—more than enough time for the victim to be dragged off into slavery or to be killed. If kept in a sealed container, the poison will remain potent for a year or so but will degrade in sixty days once it's exposed to air or light. It can be dissolved with alcohol.

THE JUICER

A "goblin trap" devised by the dwarves of Mithral Hall, this rolling device of stone and steel is assembled in the tunnels and used to mow down the hapless humanoids who dare to attack Mithral Hall from below. The dwarves of Mithral Hall will become famous in the ensuing years for their elaborate traps and defensive devices that fire multiple arrows or fling fireballs at anyone who risks entering the halls of Clan Battlehammer uninvited.

THE LEGEND OF DRIZZT BOOK VIII
STARLESS NIGHT

Drizzt had spent nearly two-thirds of his life in the Underdark, and a good portion of the last twenty years underground in the caverns of Clan Battlehammer. This was the land of starless nights—no, not nights, just a single, unending starless night, Drizzt decided—of stagnant air, and leering stalactites.

Still grieving from the death of valiant Wulfgar, Drizzt, Catti-brie, Regis, and Bruenor get wind of drow massing in the deep caverns beneath Mithral Hall. Hoping to prevent an attack, Drizzt sets out alone for a place he thought he'd never go back to: Menzoberranzan.

Catti-brie, after learning from Regis of Drizzt's plans, goes off after the dark elf. Still shaken by Wulfgar's death, Bruenor is further distressed by Drizzt and Catti-brie's departure and falls into a deep melancholy. Regis is left to plan the defense of Mithral Hall with General Dagna and Thibbledorf Pwent.

On his way to Menzoberranzan, Drizzt encounters a group of elves and recognizes one of them as the young elf he saved many years before from his own drow patrol.

Catti-brie and Guenhwyvar are once more at his side when Drizzt reaches the City of Spiders. But Menzoberranzan is as dangerous a place as ever, and they're quickly captured by Jarlaxle on the Isle of

Rothé. Jarlaxle is the leader of Bregan D'aerthe, a band of mercenaries. Drizzt and Catti-brie, to their surprise, discover that Artemis Entreri is not only alive but has come to live in the drow city.

Seeking to complete a task at which Drizzt's own mother failed, Matron Mother Baenre plans to sacrifice Drizzt to the vile spider goddess, Lolth—but Jarlaxle has plans of his own. The mercenary allows Drizzt and Catti-brie to escape, and Entreri realizes that the two may be his only ticket out of the drow city. The three of them reluctantly join forces, but Jarlaxle stays behind.

Drizzt encounters two rivals from his past: Dantrag Baenre and his brother Berg'inyon Baenre. Defeating Dantrag just as Catti-brie destroys the Baenre chapel, Drizzt leads the unlikely trio out of the city and through the treacherous Underdark.

Back on the surface, Entreri goes off on his own. For now, the truce will hold, but it won't hold forever.

1 | ETERNAL ENEMIES

Never have two master swordsmen been so evenly matched in skill and cunning but so different in temperament and outlook. The selfish and morally bankrupt Artemis Entreri grew up on the streets of Calimport, where he had to fight to survive. The thieves and lowlifes of the overcrowded city quickly identified his skill at arms, and soon enough Entreri was the most effective and highest-paid assassin in Calimport.Drizzt grew up in a no less difficult place, the drow city of Menzoberranzan, and also had to fight to survive his childhood. But under the tutelage of first Zaknafein then Montolio, Drizzt developed a conscience and compassion that Entreri rejects. Evenly matched in skill, strength, and agility, only their choices will determine who will finally prevail.

ISLE OF ROTHÉ

Less than a hundred yards long and half that wide, the Isle of Rothé rests in the calm waters of Donigarten Lake, far on the eastern edge of Menzoberranzan. The broken landscape is overgrown with strange varieties of fungi and mosses upon which the rothé herds graze. The cattlelike beasts are a primary food source for the city and are tended by orc slaves.

THE LEGEND OF DRIZZT BOOK IX
SIEGE OF DARKNESS

Guenhwyvar's ears went flat again, and the panther slipped silently into the darkness. The friends, feeling suddenly weary of it all, moved into position and were relieved indeed when the newest group rambled into sight. No drow this time, no kobolds or minotaurs. A column of dwarves, more than a score, hailed them and approached.

Mithral Hall braces for invasion from the drow massing deep in the Underdark. Drizzt and Catti-brie are dispatched to Settlestone to seek the aid of Berkthgar, while Matron Baenre works to solidify the alliances she needs with the other Houses of Menzoberranzan.

In Settlestone, Catti-brie ends up challenging Berkthgar, and after a long fight, Berkthgar agrees to assist the dwarves and also declares his desire for Catti-brie.

Demons advise various dark elves of Menzoberranzan, acting as servants but also seeking to manipulate the drow. Finally, the demons stream out and surround House Oblodra.

The deep gnomes of Blingdenstone, afraid they'll be caught between the drow and the dwarves, summon an elemental prince to defend them.

The Harpell mages arrive in Mithral Hall. Drizzt finds Catti-brie and tests her to see whether or not she has mastered her magical sword, which they've discovered is sentient—and evil.

Matron Baenre destroys House Oblodra with the assistance of Errtu, and eventually the drow march from Menzoberranzan. Passing through Blingdenstone, they find the svirfneblin city deserted.

Mithral Hall's plight soon attracts defenders from the neighboring communities of Longsaddle, Settlestone, Silverymoon, and Nesmé—and the fight for Mithral Hall is joined.

Drizzt and his friends, with the Harpell mages and the Gutbuster Brigade, advance on the drow positions and do battle with their humanoid slaves. Svirfneblin agents align themselves with the dwarves, seeing the dark elves as a common enemy.

Exploring the ancient tunnels in the deepest reaches of Mithral Hall, the drow spread their attack over numerous fronts, drow warriors and their slaves clashing with barbarians, and drow lizard riders battling Silverymoon's Knights in Silver.

Drizzt, Catti-brie, Bruenor, Guenhwyvar, and Regis take the fight directly to the leaders of the drow army. The battle rages and lives are lost on both sides, with magic and axes flashing in the dimly lit recesses of the Underdark.

But the duplicitous drow of the City of Spiders prove to be their own worst enemies, turning on each other when the opportunity arises. Matron Baenre finds she has as many enemies among the dark elves as she does among the dwarves, and Drizzt and his comrades take full advantage of her situation.

In the end, though demons take the field and good friends breathe their last, Drizzt, Bruenor, and the dwarves of Mithral Hall drive the invading drow out of their tunnels and find an unlikely alliance with the deep gnomes of abandoned Blingdenstone.

1 SPELLWEB

A spell granted by Lolth to her evil priestesses, the spellweb is a mass of sticky webs that glows with a green luminescence. The snare has to be anchored to two or more points—easy enough to do in the stalagmite-riddled floor of an Underdark cavern. The weight of the webs can hold a victim fast, making it nearly impossible to move. A victim's only hope is to be nimble enough on his feet to leap away before the webs fully form.

2 SUMMONING A DEMON

Only the most powerful clerics or mages have both the ability and the courage—or, some would say, hubris—to even attempt to summon a demon from the endless Abyss. To do so requires a complex spell that first opens a gateway between planes (a circle of arcane or divine light as wide as twenty feet in diameter) that allows the summoner to call across the multiverse to attract the attention of a particular demonic creature.

Though he can't necessarily be certain he's called the right creature, something will inevitably answer, and the priest or wizard will have to hope he's prepared for the struggle necessary to exert his control over the being of pure evil that steps through.

RIDING LIZARDS

The dark elves of Menzoberranzan and elsewhere have tamed enormous subterranean lizards to use as mounts. These horse-sized reptiles can cling to vertical surfaces and are able to walk as easily on the walls or even the ceiling of a cavern as they do on the floor. Most of the noble Houses of the City of Spiders maintain a troop of highly trained male lizard riders as their elite cavalry.

THE LEGEND OF DRIZZT BOOK X
PASSAGE TO DAWN

ErItu, a creature of the fiery Abyss, was no friend of snow and ice, but the texture of the great icebergs clogging the waters—a mountain range built among defensible, freezing moats—showed him potential he could not resist.

The monstrous demon Errtu plots his return from the Abyss to exact his revenge on Drizzt. Unaware of the demon's plans, Drizzt and Catti-brie travel with Captain Deudermont aboard the pirate-hunter *Sea Sprite*.

Still in the smoldering Abyss, Errtu lures *Sea Sprite* to a mysterious island in the Sea of Swords, an island inhabited by a malevolent witch. The witch is in the employ of Errtu and helps to further lure Drizzt into the demon's hands, teasing him with an incomprehensible verse.

Meanwhile, Bruenor and Regis return to Icewind Dale to meet with the barbarian leader Berkthgar. Berkthgar hopes to see the barbarians return to their traditional ways, once more closing themselves off from the folk of Ten-Towns and from the dwarves of Mithral Hall.

Back on the island, Drizzt puzzles over the witch's enigmatic verse. With the help of the wizard Harkle Harpell, Drizzt and *Sea Sprite* travel to an inland lake near the Spirit Soaring. There they meet the priest Cadderly, who helps Drizzt decode the witch's message—but Cadderly unwittingly frees the demon in the process.

Drizzt and Catti-brie return to Icewind Dale with Cadderly's help and are surprised to find the tensions between the barbarians and the dwarves so high.

A dwarf named Stumpet uncovers the Crystal Shard, lost in an avalanche so long ago. The vile sentient artifact immediately goes to work on poor Stumpet's will.

No sooner has Drizzt reunited with his friends than Errtu appears in Icewind Dale, taking the Crystal Shard from Stumpet and imprisoning her soul. Errtu raises his crystal tower on the treacherous ice floes of the Sea of Moving Ice.

Battling not only Errtu and his demonic minions but the freezing dangers of the chaotic ice floes, Drizzt and his comrades engage Errtu. The biggest surprise of the battle comes when Drizzt finds the soul of fallen Wulfgar, which has been trapped by the vengeful demon. They manage to release Wulfgar from his hellish imprisonment, and the raging barbarian helps them defeat the demon that has tortured him for so long.

With Errtu finally defeated, the only thing left is to deal, once and for all, with Crenshinibon. . . .

1 MANES

Sub-demons that fill the very bottom ranks of the Abyssal Hordes, manes are created from the souls of the dead who, in life, were both evil and weak. Greater demons are known to feed on them and keep thousands as slaves and footsoldiers. Killing one reduces it to a greasy cloud of reeking gas—but there will always be more where they came from.

2 THE SEA OF MOVING ICE

The Sea of Moving Ice lies at the far northwest edge of the mapped continent of Faerûn, directly west of Icewind Dale and Ten-Towns. The great ice islands—some stationary, some flat ice floes, others towering bergs—never melt and constantly shift on the currents of the northern Sea of Swords. Only the most foolish captains brave the ice floes, and many ships remain frozen in place for decades—and many more are immediately dashed to splinters.

3 MARILITHS

These serpentine, six-armed demons serve as lieutenants for more powerful demons (like the balor Errtu). Mariliths are highly intelligent and cunning creatures who are as comfortable devising grand strategies as they are slicing at their opponents with as many as six exotic bladed weapons at a time. Their snakelike bodies can wrap around a victim and squeeze the life right out of him, and their inherent magical abilities make them more than a match for Faerûn's bravest defenders.

THE LEGEND OF DRIZZT BOOK XI
THE SILENT BLADE

"I've no intention of turning back," Drizzt said. "Not yet. Not until we have proof that these tracks foretell a greater disaster than one, or even a handful, of giants could perpetrate."

Drizzt, Catti-brie, Bruenor, Regis, and Wulfgar travel to the Spirit Soaring to ask for Cadderly's help in destroying the Crystal Shard. All manner of dangerous creatures, called by the evil of Crenshinibon, follow Drizzt and his companions.

Wulfgar is deeply troubled by thoughts of his time as Errtu's prisoner in the Abyss. He can't hold back the painful memories, though, and ends up striking Catti-brie. Ashamed, Wulfgar leaves his friends to set out on his own.

Artemis Entreri returns to Calimport, and the city's various thieves' guilds watch his every move. He renews old contacts but hears that Pasha Basadoni has threatened anyone who works with Entreri—Basadoni wants the assassin either as an exclusive member of his guild or dead, and other assassins target Entreri to prove their own skills.

Alone in the North, Wulfgar once again encounters the Sky Pony tribe and kills the shaman who once tried to kill him. Still tormented, he ends up in Luskan where he takes a job as a bouncer in the Cutlass, a dockside tavern.

Down in Calimport, Entreri is contacted by Jarlaxle, who seeks to renew their partnership. Entreri only agrees when Jarlaxle guarantees to arrange another meeting between the assassin and Drizzt. But first, Entreri has to get Pasha Basadoni out of the way, and he does so with the aid of a gang of wererats.

Continuing on their way to the Spirit Soaring, Drizzt, Bruenor, Catti-brie, and Regis take a riverboat crewed by dwarf brothers. They're attacked by goblins, and Regis is badly injured. Two priests, one who claims to be Cadderly, find them and offer assistance. Drizzt gives "Cadderly" the Crystal Shard, not knowing that the priest is actually one of Jarlaxle's agents in disguise, sent to lure Drizzt to his meeting with Entreri.

Jarlaxle uses Crenshinibon to raise a crystal tower, attracting Drizzt. Within the tower, Drizzt and Entreri once more face off, for what both believe will be their final duel. But Jarlaxle only wants Entreri to finally get his obsession with Drizzt out of his system so the two can get down to business. With the help of a Bregan D'aerthe psionicist, Entreri is led to believe that he's killed Drizzt.

Drizzt is healed and allowed to leave, as long as Jarlaxle is able to keep the Crystal Shard. Though Drizzt is hardly happy to see the powerful evil artifact fall into drow hands, at least he knows it will only further corrupt the already depraved City of Spiders.

1 *BOTTOM FEEDER*

Bottom Feeder is a river boat owned by Bumpo Thunderpuncher. His brother Donat and the dwarf cousins Yipper and Quipper Fishquisher help crew the boat. Though it's not entirely unheard of for dwarves to operate riverboats and barges, it is quite rare. Dwarves don't tend to be big fans of water.

2 TRACKING

Drizzt learned to track people and monsters over most types of terrain as part of his training with Montolio. Depending on the terrain, tracking quarry can be easy or very difficult. Soft ground makes footprints and other signs easier to see, and the harder the ground, the more difficult it is to stay on track. But a ranger like Drizzt is trained to look for more than footprints. Blood trails, a stray hair, or clumps of fur . . . even a loose button that falls from a garment can show an experienced tracker the path to his intended target.

The rest of the Cutlass's patrons stared at the row in amusement and confusion, for they knew that Wulfgar worked for Arumn. The only ones moving were skidding safely out of range of the whirling ball of brawlers. One man in the far corner stood up, waving his arms wildly and spinning in circles.

Wulfgar is in the port city of Luskan, where he's befriended Morik the Rogue, a local thief. The once-proud barbarian has sunk into despair, turning to the bottle for solace and working as a bouncer at the Cutlass. He's also become close with Delly Curtie, one of the Cutlass's barmaids.

Captain Deudermont has brought *Sea Sprite* to port in Luskan, though his wizard, Robillard, and other members of his crew despise the city—a notorious den of pirates and rogues. Deudermont sees Wulfgar at the Cutlass and is shocked to see that he has fallen so far, so fast. Wulfgar pretends not to know Deudermont.

Meanwhile, in the remote mountain fiefdom of Auckney, Meralda, the teenaged daughter of a local farmer, swoons over a peasant boy named Jaka Sculi. But Feringal, the Lord of Auckney, has his sights set on the beautiful Meralda. Despite his sister Priscilla's arguments to the contrary, Feringal pursues the reluctant Meralda, who all but throws herself at Jaka. Lord Feringal asks for Meralda's hand in marriage. Meralda's mother is sick and her family poor, so Meralda can hardly refuse the marriage, but her heart is still with Jaka.

Wulfgar continues to spiral down, sinking so low that a local cutpurse is able to steal Aegis-fang while Wulfgar lies in a drunken stupor. The thief sells the hammer to a pirate captain named Sheila Kree.

The pirate thugs Creeps Sharky and Tee-a-nicknick, a half-qullan, attempt to assassinate Captain Deudermont to collect a bounty, but Wulfgar and Morik are accused of the crime. Even though Deudermont survives the attack, Wulfgar and Morik end up at Prisoners' Carnival, where they're to be publicly tortured to death. But Deudermont intervenes on their behalf, and Wulfgar and Morik are allowed to live but are exiled from the city.

In Auckney, Meralda finally agrees to marry Lord Feringal, and at the wedding, Jaka accidentally kills himself, leaving a distraught Meralda with a secret—a pregnancy she can still hide, but not for long.

Wulfgar and Morik travel to the dangerous North, fighting through the wilderness and finally making their way—by accident—to Auckney. By that time they've become highwaymen, and when they waylay the coach in which Meralda is riding, the young girl sees her chance. She accuses Wulfgar of raping her, a convenient explanation for her ill-timed pregnancy.

Once again accused of a crime he didn't commit, Wulfgar later ends up saving Meralda's baby, a girl named Colson, from the clutches of Lord Feringal's sister. Once Feringal learns that Wulfgar is not the father of the baby and is innocent of the charges brought against him by Meralda, he allows Wulfgar to leave with the baby.

Having taken on responsibility for Colson, Wulfgar climbs out of the bottle, returns to Luskan for Delly, and goes out in search of Aegis-fang.

① QULLANS

Exotic humanoids from distant jungle lands, qullans wear elaborate tattoos, war paint, and ritual scars. They're fierce fighters but are disorganized and chaotic in the extreme. An aura of confusion radiates from them that makes their opponents flail madly around and attack their own allies or simply stand still wondering where they are and what's going on. Their masterwork broadswords have to be meticulously maintained, having been forged from an unknown alloy that tends to blunt as they fight. Though they avoid contact with humans, it is possible for humans and qullans to breed with each other.

② THE CUTLASS

This seaside tavern on Half-Moon Street in Luskan is a popular hangout for sailors of every stripe. A table full of pirate thugs in the corner, a group of whalers over by the fire, and the crew of a legitimate merchantman at the bar all drink—and, as often as not, brawl—together at the Cutlass. The owner, Arumn Gardpeck, is practical enough to turn a blind eye when necessary but stern enough to do what he must to maintain order in his establishment—like hiring Wulfgar as his bouncer.

THE LEGEND OF DRIZZT BOOK XIII
SEA OF SWORDS

With nothing but open water ahead, the ship had no chance of escape. No vessel on the Sword Coast could outrun Sea Sprite, especially with the powerful wizard Robillard sitting atop the back of the flying bridge, summoning gusts of wind repeatedly into the schooner's mainsail.

A strange elf named Le'lorinel is training to fight against an opponent armed with two swords—and has vowed to kill Drizzt Do'Urden.

Though they still wonder what's become of Wulfgar, the rest of the friends—Drizzt, Catti-brie, Bruenor, and Regis—have found peace in Icewind Dale. But that peace is interrupted by a band of highwaymen led by the wily Jule Pepper, who surrenders when faced down by Guenhwyvar.

Wulfgar has joined Captain Deudermont's crew and helps them hunt pirates in hopes of encountering Sheila Kree and retrieving Aegis-fang. Sheila Kree has used the markings on the side of the hammer to brand herself and her most loyal crewmembers. When Jule Pepper stands trial, that brand is revealed, and Drizzt and his friends realize that Aegis-fang is no longer in Wulfgar's hands. Fearing the worst, Drizzt and Catti-brie set off to find either their friend or his warhammer.

Wulfgar returns to Waterdeep, *Sea Sprite'* s home port, where Delly and Colson are staying at Deudermont's lavish house. The barbarian is torn between his new responsibilities as a family man and his need to reclaim Aegis-fang.

Le'lorinel continues to hunt Drizzt and goes to Luskan, where Drizzt and Catti-brie are trying to catch up with Wulfgar. They hear the story of his exile and discover that Aegis-fang has been sold to Sheila Kree. Le'lorinel

is shanghaied in Luskan and brought to Sheila's hideout at Golden Cove, while Bruenor and Regis set out to meet Drizzt and Catti-brie.

Gayselle, one of Sheila Kree's hired killers, is sent to Waterdeep to kill Deudermont but finds Delly and Colson instead. But Drizzt and Catti-brie have also come to Waterdeep, and they save Delly and the baby from the pirates.

Wulfgar is still out at sea aboard *Sea Sprite*, and Drizzt and Catti-brie decide to go back to Luskan, where they meet up with Bruenor and Regis. They now know that Wulfgar is going after Aegis-fang, and they're determined to help him. They travel north, passing through Auckney, and hear the rest of the tale of the exiled Wulfgar.

Eventually, all roads meet at Golden Cove, the cavern complex that Sheila shares with the ogres of Clan Thump. Le'lorinel, who has become a member of Sheila's crew, faces down Drizzt and is killed. Only then does Drizzt realize that Le'lorinel is actually Ellifain, the elf girl he saved many years before. Drizzt is almost overcome with grief.

Wulfgar, once more fighting side-by-side with his friends, regains Aegis-fang, and together they defeat Sheila and her pirates. But their emotional reunion is interrupted by news that Gandalug Battlehammer has died, and Bruenor must return to Mithral Hall to once more serve as king.

FRIENDS REUNITED

The Companions of the Hall have experienced a great deal of strife and heartache, but even powerful demons and gods can't keep them apart forever. Together once more, they will return to Mithral Hall and face new challenges from an orc king who will unite the squabbling tribes of the Spine of the World and bring out the hunter in Drizzt. The Legend of Drizzt has come to an end, but the story is far from over.

PEOPLE OF THE LEGEND OF DRIZZT

Catti-brie's mind drifted from her friends, back to Icewind Dale, to the rocky mountain, Kelvin's Cairn, dotting the otherwise flat tundra. It was so similar to this very place. Colder, perhaps, but the air held the same crispness, the same clear, vital texture. How far she and her friends, Drizzt and Guenhwyvar, Bruenor and Regis, and of course, Wulfgar, had come from that place! And in so short a time! A frenzy of adventures, a lifetime of excitement and thrills and good deeds. Together they were an unbeatable force.

So they had thought.

—Siege of Darkness

DRIZZT DO'URDEN

Drizzt Do'Urden trotted along silently, his soft, low-cut boots barely stirring the dust. He kept the cowl of his brown cloak pulled low over the flowing waves of his stark white hair and moved with such effortless grace that an onlooker might have thought him to be no more than an illusion, an optical trick of the brown sea of tundra.

—*The Crystal Shard*

Drizzt Do'Urden is a drow from the Underdark city of Menzoberranzan, the third son of Matron Mother Malice of House Do'Urden. He is born on the eve of battle in the Year of the Singing Skull (1297 DR), and the Legend of Drizzt follows his life from birth to the age of seventy-four (still young for an elf) in the Year of the Tankard (1370 DR).

Like all dark elves, Drizzt has pitch black skin and white hair, but his lavender eyes—which gleam with feral light before he wades into battle—set him apart from most drow, whose eyes are typically red. His eyes have become accustomed to sunlight but are attuned to darkness, and his hearing is almost supernaturally keen. At somewhere between five and five-and-a-half feet tall, Drizzt is surprisingly small, slender, and light, but anyone who thinks that means he isn't dangerous probably won't live to make the same mistake again. Though he eventually loses his innate ability to levitate, he shares the remaining magical talents of his kin.

Having run from his home in the City of Spiders, Drizzt comes to the World Above a renegade, a stranger in a land where his kind are seen—rightfully so—as evil beings from a world of darkness and evil. Though he lives for a time in a cave on the slopes of Kelvin's Cairn, he eventually finds a home with his friends in the dwarven city of Mithral Hall, and for the longest time, Drizzt is sure he is the only drow living on the surface.

A man of integrity and honor, he flies in the face of everything it means to be a drow. Though he is born in a city where treachery is the rule of the day, Drizzt tries to keep his word, however dangerous it might be for him. His personality and ethics are so strong that even the gruff and suspicious Bruenor Battlehammer uses Drizzt as inspiration for the dwarves in his charge.

More than a paradigm of honor and integrity, Drizzt is an excellent deductive thinker, with a steady, logical mind that never folds under pressure, though he will sometimes rely on instinct in critical situations. On a day-to-day basis, Drizzt is a stoic, calm, and serious individual, but he's always thinking—thinking about his place in the world, the value of his friendships, and the truth of his elf's longevity that will see him outlive all of his closest friends.

Though he honors Mielikki above all other gods, he has an almost agnostic outlook where the godly powers are concerned.

INNATE MAGICAL ABILITIES

Drizzt shares the same innate magical abilities that all drow possess. With merely a thought—a reflex—drow are able to summon a globe of impenetrable darkness, blinding those inside it, even those with the keenest eyesight. Conversely, they can also set an opponent aglow with shimmering faerie fire, an enchanted glow that makes picking out a target in subterranean darkness much easier. Dark elves are also able to levitate, lifting up into the air or floating down from great heights. This is truly advantageous in the three-dimensional world of the Underdark, so full of pits and shafts.

Since most creatures of the Underdark are attracted to any light, the drow ability to conjure dancing lights—little floating points of illumination—can serve to attract or distract prey. Drow themselves are sensitive to bright lights, their eyes having adapted to life in the Underdark. They see better in darkness than any of their elf cousins from the World Above.

THE UNDERDARK

A world-spanning network of caverns, tunnels, and vaults, the Underdark is home to millions of sentient creatures and millions more terrifying creatures out of the darkest nightmares. Few surface dwellers have the courage to travel there, and fewer still would be able to find a way to "live off the land." Food can be found, and water is plentiful, but most of any Underdark traveler's time is spent not eating but trying not to be eaten.

Drizzt learns a wide range of skills, including his two-handed fighting style, from the drow of House Do'Urden and the military academy of Melee-Magthere in Menzoberranzan.

He also spends some time at Sorcere, a school for drow wizards, where he learns to recognize various forms of spellcraft and is made familiar with the different planes of existence that make up the infinite multiverse. Drizzt can sense the presence of a being from the lower planes or the beginning of a spell directed at him, and he can even attune his senses to a magical item to gain information about it.

When he comes to the surface, he learns more—the ways of the ranger, how to decode the battle drums of the barbarians, and even how to navigate the World Above by the sun and stars.

But most impressive of all is Drizzt's skill as a fighter. His balance, speed, and agility are all superior to those of most of his opponents, even other drow. Possessed of keen senses, Drizzt is almost unnaturally perceptive and nearly impossible to surprise.

Protected by magical armor in the form of a mithral shirt, Drizzt tends to cover himself with a simple black, gray, or

forest green hooded cloak that he uses to hide his drow features from less receptive surface dwellers. In addition to his pair of enchanted scimitars, Twinkle and Icingdeath, Drizzt is rarely without at least one dagger, a weapon he can throw with considerable accuracy.

Around his neck is a unicorn pendant that was carved for him by Regis, and serves as his tie to the nature goddess Mielikki.

Drizzt has used a magical mask in the past that allows him to disguise himself, most often as a surface elf. Though he isn't always comfortable using the mask for fear he might lose himself in the illusion, he's a smart and sophisticated tactical thinker and takes risks when he needs to. Magical anklets lend him even more speed and greater balance, and then there's the onyx figurine of a panther that he never leaves behind. . . .

SCIMITARS

These long swords have curved blades with the edge on the convex side. Used throughout the Realms since time immemorial, they originated in the far-off land of Zakhara. The name is thought to come from an early description of the weapon: "the lion's claw," or *šimšīr*, in the language of those mysterious southerners. Scimitars are known for their speed in combat, and the curved blade allows the wielder to parry at unexpected angles. Scimitars are notoriously difficult weapons to master.

ICINGDEATH

Plundered from the lair of the great white wyrm Ingeloakastimizilian, also known as Dracos Icingdeath, this enchanted scimitar has a silver blade with a diamond edge. The weapon was fashioned by a Zakharan master weaponsmith whose name has been lost to the ages. It was eventually sold to an archwizard of ancient Netheril and enchanted so that it protects its owner from fire. Drizzt fights with Icingdeath in his right hand.

TWINKLE

In Drizzt's left hand is Twinkle, a perfectly balanced scimitar given to him by the wizard Malchor Harpell. The razor-edged blade was forged by the elves of Siluvanede, who set in its pommel a star-cut blue sapphire. When the sword's name is spoken, it glows with an eerie blue light and surges with arcane power.

MASK OF DISGUISE

Once guarded by the banshee Agatha, this enchanted item appears to be an unremarkable mask with simple features. It has but a single strap to secure it to the wearer's head. When it covers Drizzt's face, he feels a tingling sensation as the magic takes hold, and though he otherwise feels no different, to anyone looking at him his appearance changes completely. The mask disappears, and what's left is a whole new face, its features limited only by the imagination of the wearer. Because it can slip off in combat, the mask is best used for the careful infiltration of guarded spaces or the non-violent manipulation of an unsuspecting victim.

GUENHWYVAR

A mist came up, swirling about the figurine, growing thicker and thicker, flowing and swirling and taking the shape of the great panther. Thicker and thicker, and then it was no mist circling the onyx likeness, but the panther herself. Guenhwyvar looked up at Drizzt with eyes showing an intelligence far beyond that indicated by her feline form.

—The Silent Blade

More than three times the size of an ordinary panther, the great black cat Guenhwyvar is six hundred pounds of silent power. Her head—with green eyes the size of saucers—is as wide as Drizzt's shoulders, and her mighty paws could cover a man's face. Gifted with incredible speed and strength, the panther can leap across distances of twenty feet or more. But the cat is not just a physical powerhouse; she's also a cunning and intelligent hunter.

Different from other panthers in more than just her size, Guenhwyvar is actually a denizen of the endless expanse of the Astral Plane, called into being on the Prime Material by use of a beautifully carved onyx figurine. Whoever possesses the figurine can call Guenhwyvar from the Astral by holding the figurine and speaking her name.

Guenhwyvar hears the call and sees a flash of light, then travels through a planar tunnel to the figurine. A gray mist coalesces around the figurine then solidifies into the black cat. Though Guenhwyvar can return to the Astral Plane at will, she can only be called to the Prime Material by use of the figurine, and once called, she is compelled—under all but the most extreme circumstances—to obey the commands of her summoner. The cat can be held back by the same magic circles used to protect summoners from demons and other extraplanar creatures.

When Guenhwyvar is sent back to the Astral Plane, she walks in circles around the figurine and fades away into the same gray mist. Once back on her home plane, she's rejuvenated and heals completely, even from mortal wounds, as is the case when Pasha Pook kills her. She can only stay on the Prime Material Plane for half a day out of every two.

It's also possible to travel the planes with her, and Drizzt has done so in the past. If the figurine and the cat are on the Astral Plane together, Guenhwyvar and the holder of the figurine can go anywhere in the multiverse from there.

The onyx figurine is currently in the possession of Drizzt, and the drow wizard Masoj Hun'ett possessed it before him. But the figurine changed hands many, many times before that. It was enchanted by the human wizard Anders Beltgarden in the Year of Somber Smiles (253 DR), more than a thousand years before it came into Drizzt's possession. Anders's friend, the elf bladesinger Josidiah Starym, gave the cat her name.

More than just a magic item, a pet, or a weapon, Guenhwyvar has become a true friend of Drizzt, who often calls her "Guen."

FIGURINES OF WONDROUS POWER

The onyx figurine that calls Guenhwyvar to the Prime Material Plane is unique among a class of magic items known to the mages of the Realms as figurines of wondrous power. More common are the Bronze Griffon, the Ebony Fly, the Golden Lion, the Ivory Goats (of which there are three distinct types: the Goat of Traveling, the Goat of Travail, and the Goat of Terror), the Marble Elephant, the Onyx Dog, the Silver Raven, and the Obsidian Steed.

Each of these figurines will call into being the animal depicted. All are either larger than average (the Ebony Fly, for instance, is the size of pony when animated and can even be ridden) or have some magical ability that sets them apart.

CATTI-BRIE

Taulmaril twanged once, again, and then a third time, Catti-brie blasting holes in the ranks. She used the sudden and deadly explosions of streaking lines and sparks as cover and ran, not away, as she knew the goblins would expect, but straight ahead, backtracking along her original route.

—Starless Night

The so-called Princess of Mithral Hall, Catti-brie was raised by dwarves to fight and work, work and fight. She's one-hundred-and-thirty pounds of muscle.

When her parents are killed in a goblin raid on the town of Termalaine, the young Catti-brie is rescued by the dwarf king Bruenor Battlehammer, who takes her in and raises her as his own daughter. Their family bond is as strong as it is unlikely, and in some ways, Catti-brie is more dwarf than human and is fiercely devoted to Clan Battlehammer.

Born in the Year of the Weeping Moon (1339 DR), she's the same age as Wulfgar, who also was taken in by Bruenor. Though they may have been raised by the same adoptive father, her love for Wulfgar runs deep, and as they grow up, they eventually plan to marry. But Catti-brie's suppressed feelings for Drizzt—and his for her—threaten to tear all three of them apart. Still she considers Drizzt her dearest friend, and Catti-brie may well know him better than anyone else in the world.

Catti-brie's pleasant, lyrical voice is offset by the Dwarvish brogue she inherited from her father and the other dwarves of Clan Battlehammer, and her blue eyes sparkle with an innocent, almost girlish joy. Her sense of humor is also informed by her time spent with Bruenor, and she can keep her chin up even when wounded.

TAULMARIL

The fabled Heartseeker, this enchanted bow is accompanied by a quiver of silver arrows that streak to their target leaving a trail of blinding light behind them. When the arrow strikes its target, a shower of multicolored sparks bursts forth, and all but the most powerful foes are instantly destroyed. It's as though Taulmaril fires lightning, not arrows. The bow once hung in a chamber honoring dwarf heroes from the first age of Mithral Hall. Its accompanying quiver never runs out of arrows. In the hands of as accomplished an archer as Catti-brie, this is a deadly weapon indeed.

KHAZID'HEA

Catti-brie's magical sword is also called "Cutter." Possessed of a sentience all its own, Khazid'hea thirsts for blood and demands to be fed. Catti-brie is only barely able to overcome the sword's influence, but not everyone who's held it has been so lucky. It has served many masters and has been master to many more, since its demonic intelligence was forced into the form of a sword deep in the pits of the Abyss four thousand years ago.

Its blade is sharp enough to cut stone and never dulls, the edge glowing with a line of red light so thin that it's barely perceptible. When it was in the dark elf Dantrag Baenre's possession, the pommel was sculpted in the shape of a demon with rubies for eyes, but the sword is able to change the appearance of its pommel to whatever shape it feels will best attract its chosen wielder. For Drizzt, it forms into a white-metal likeness of a unicorn. No one who knows Khazid'hea well is fooled by that apparently harmless disguise.

With a zest for life that seems to know no bounds, Catti-brie loves the open road, always seeking out new experiences. If she thinks someone needs a moment of clarity, she isn't above giving him a slap to the back of the head. Though she may not appreciate stubbornness in others, she can be intractable in her thinking, occasionally harsh and commanding, but underlying all of that is a sincere sensitivity.

Her courage has never been brought into question, and Catti-brie has never shied from a fight. Only once has she been truly terrified, and that was at the hands of the assassin Artemis Entreri. She carries the memory of that encounter with her like a deep wound that she's allowed no one to see. Her willingness to sacrifice herself for her friends and her ability to fight on even in the most hopeless circumstances are an inspiration to those around her.

Trained in the martial arts by Bruenor himself, Catti-brie is an accomplished fighter and talented archer, but sometimes she has difficulty coordinating her actions with others. Though not as agile as a drow, she's nimble and sure-footed.

Catti-brie fights with the sentient sword Khazid'hea and with Taulmaril, the magic bow of Anariel that she recovered from the ruins of Mithral Hall. She wears a thin, supple coat of finely crafted dwarven mithral chain mail under a gray cloak. The cat's eye agate on a slim, silver chain that she wears around her head was given to her by Alustriel of Silverymoon. It gives her the ability to see in the dark almost as well as a drow.

WULFGAR

"I lost Aegis-fang through my own fault," he admitted, which of course everyone already knew. "And now I understand the error—my error. And so I will go after the warhammer as soon as I may, through sleet and snow, against dragons and pirates alike if need be."

—Sea of Swords

Wulfgar, son of Beornegar, stands seven feet tall and is easily twice Drizzt's weight. His fair skin and blue eyes betray his northern heritage. Though he is normally clean shaven, the barbarian has slipped into long periods of depression, the depth of which can be measured by the length of his beard.

The same age as Catti-brie, Wulfgar was also raised by the dwarf king Bruenor. Instead of being rescued in a raid, the young barbarian was captured and held for five years as a captive of Clan Battlehammer. Over those five years, the young barbarian and the gruff old dwarf became like father and son.

Wulfgar spent the first part of his childhood with the Tribe of the Elk, one of the wandering clans of the Uthgardt barbarians. After his capture, he became as much a dwarf as a human, toiling in the Battlehammer mines in Icewind Dale. That upbringing has made him an honorable and powerful man but also has left him rather naive in the ways of "civilized" men. His discomfort with cities and their customs is only outweighed by his burning curiosity and wanderlust.

Trained in hand-to-hand combat by Drizzt Do'Urden, and armed with the powerful enchanted warhammer Aegis-fang, Wulfgar is a formidable fighter. Despite his time with the dwarves, he continues to revere the war god Tempus the Foehammer. Even so, Wulfgar has grown beyond his barbarian ancestry to become a skilled weaponsmith and an intelligent, thoughtful young man.

During an effort to rescue Catti-brie from a terrifying yochlol, Wulfgar is buried in a cave-in and is presumed dead. But the yochlol drags him into the Abyss and gives him to the balor Errtu. For six years Wulfgar suffers horrific torture at the hands of Errtu and his demonic minions. Though he is eventually rescued and

returned to Faerûn, the young barbarian is scarred in ways his friends cannot understand, and the once vibrant and spirited warrior slips into a deep, self-destructive depression. He chooses to hide in the bottom of a bottle, but eventually the will he was born with and that was nurtured by the likes of Bruenor and Drizzt wins out, and Wulfgar struggles back to regain his dignity and his birthright.

Perhaps most tragic of all is Wulfgar's interrupted engagement to Catti-brie. They truly love each other and intended to marry, but when Wulfgar is presumed killed by the yochlol, Catti-brie has to move on—to the arms of Drizzt.

It has taken quite some time for Wulfgar to shed some of the superstitions of his barbarian upbringing. Once deeply suspicious, even fearful, of wizards and magic, Wulfgar has begun to embrace those who practice the Art. Still, he can be naive at times and is easily embarrassed by aggressive women, overly articulate city-dwellers, and those who risk prying into his private thoughts.

He maintains the strict code of honor of his ancestors and reacts very strongly when confronted with dishonorable behavior in others. It's difficult for Wulfgar even to understand when someone is being deceitful. The full fury of his temper, which can often get the better of him, is reserved for those who prey on the weak. Wulfgar will never back down in the face of a bully and will not stand for torture or the mistreatment of women and children.

The barbarian is strong enough to lift the weight of three average men over his head, and he lifted a full-grown camel off the ground and thrown it. His approach to combat tends to be rather direct, bashing away with warhammer and fists. Though he can strike with blinding speed, Wulfgar is not nearly as agile as Drizzt or Catti-brie. He makes up for that lack of finesse with brute strength and clarity of purpose.

Wulfgar is considered an ideal specimen by his barbarian brothers for his strength of arm and character. He's learned from Drizzt to turn fear into rage, and what a powerful force is Wulfgar's anger. When fully consumed by battle frenzy, Wulfgar hardly feels pain. Then he knows only the battle before him.

THE TRIBE OF THE ELK

Not to be confused with the Elk Tribe, which is little more than a gang of bandits from the Evermoors far to the south across the Spine of the World, the Tribe of the Elk is one of only two surviving human barbarian tribes of Icewind Dale—the other is the Tribe of the Bear. Merciless warriors, the barbarians of Icewind Dale live by a strict code of honor and conduct, but that code doesn't prevent them from occasionally attacking their neighbors. Protective of their ancient ways, most of the barbarians of the Tribe of the Elk despise their "civilized" neighbors in Ten-Towns, but under the influence of certain strong personalities like Wulfgar, Drizzt, and Catti-brie, they've fought to defend the towns. What they truly love, however, is to follow the reindeer herds and to be left to themselves.

AEGIS-FANG

This mighty weapon was crafted by the hands of Bruenor Battlehammer and enchanted under a full moon on the night of the summer solstice. Its handle is an adamantite rod, and its head is a solid block of mithral carved with the symbols of the dwarf gods Moradin, Dumathoin, and Clangeddin, as well as secret symbols that give it extraordinary powers.

Too big for a dwarf, Aegis-fang is given to Wulfgar to wield, and in the barbarian's hands it is a weapon of both crushing destructive power and pinpoint precision. Wulfgar can throw the huge hammer with exceptional accuracy, and its magic then returns the weapon to Wulfgar's hands so it can never be retrieved by an enemy—and is ready for another throw or a good bludgeoning.

It has become the most honored weapon of all the barbarians of Icewind Dale, and when Wulfgar is believed dead, it is enshrined in the Hall of Dumathoin in Mithral Hall. When it briefly finds itself in the hands of the pirate captain Sheila Kree, the Companions of the Hall immediately set out to retrieve it. Aegis-fang will be in Wulfgar's hands or no one's.

BRUENOR BATTLEHAMMER

In this place Drizzt had lost Bruenor forever, or so he had thought, for he had seen the dwarf spiral down into the lightless depths on the back of a flaming dragon. He couldn't avoid a smile as the memory flowed to completion; it would take more than a dragon to kill mighty Bruenor Battlehammer!

—The Legacy

Bruenor Battlehammer is the oldest member of his clan, and every moment of that long, hard life shows in his gray-streaked red beard and in the wrinkled, leathery skin of his dour face. Though his right eye is missing, his remaining blue-gray eye sparkles with intelligence and wry humor. A terrible scar runs from his forehead to his jawbone and through that missing eye. His long pointed nose has been broken several times, and his stubby-fingered hands are gnarled from forge work and axe work alike. He stands four-and-a-half feet tall but is stronger and tougher than a creature twice his height.

A descendant of the legendary dwarf king Gandalug Battlehammer, Bruenor leads the tattered remnants of his clan on an epic quest to reclaim Mithral Hall, their ancestral home, from the clutches of the shadow dragon Shimmergloom. After two centuries mining Icewind Dale, Clan Battlehammer finally regains the underground labyrinth, and Bruenor—a few twists and turns aside—takes his place as the Eighth King of Mithral Hall.

Bruenor, like most dwarves, can be difficult to get to know, but once he befriends someone, it's a bond he'll march into the Nine Hells to maintain. He's gruff and stubborn but can get as rowdy as the rest of his kin. Bruenor uses magic in the crafting of powerful enchanted weapons like Aegis-fang but is suspicious of wizards and magical creatures like Guenhwyvar. Though fiercely loyal to his dwarf clan and their traditions and history, he was quick to adopt the humans Catti-brie and Wulfgar as his own. He hates orcs, deep gnomes, and duergar as much as the next dwarf but has found himself fighting side by side with them on more than one occasion. All these inconsistencies define Bruenor Battlehammer and make him both the quintessential dwarf and the model for the new dwarven age.

The Eighth King of Mithral Hall is a valiant leader who never shies from a fight and who puts on a brave, stoic face for those who look up to him. He values family and friends above all and is just as quick to call out the tales of the indomitable Drizzt Do'Urden as he is to cry out to the dwarf god Moradin, whose name is Bruenor's favored battle cry.

He shares his race's inherent pragmatism and is unimpressed by reputations or gossip. Though he is loath to admit it, he has a merchant's mind for facts and figures. In combat, he keeps a running count of his kills. In commerce, he keeps a tight string around his coin purse.

Though a clever, skilled, and experienced fighter, Bruenor often eschews his old and notched axe in favor of a good, old-fashioned head butt. Those who live to tell of it hope he seriously considers opting for the axe the next time around. This same lack of subtlety is evident in his almost complete lack of stealth.

His skill at arms is only surpassed by his skill as a weaponsmith, though some will say his greatest skill is as a storyteller. Bruenor knows how to tell a tale and has kept the legends of Mithral Hall, Gandalug, and Gauntlgrym alive in Clan Battlehammer for centuries.

Bruenor's notched axe and foaming-mug-emblazoned shield are always close at hand, and he values his helm, despite its missing horn, more than the crown of Mithral Hall. Other than a heavy cloak, a few flasks of oil, and a tinderbox, Bruenor doesn't tend to carry other trinkets or magic items. After all, he always has his forehead!

DWARVES

This hearty and stubborn race is equally at home above and below ground (where they're aided by their excellent darkvision) but always prefer rocky, mountainous lands. They're known throughout the Realms as skilled stonemasons, jewelers, armorers, and weaponsmiths—and as valiant, determined, and steadfast warriors possessed of a keen sense of honor and a tendency toward self-sacrifice that can at times seem self-destructive. Also prone to greed—or at least, the appearance of greed—dwarves value gold, mithral, and other precious metals, and all variety of gems, which they use to fashion some of the most highly prized armor, weapons, and works of art in all of Faerûn.

Though they stand just over four feet tall on average, a dwarf weighs as much as a six-foot-tall human. This combination makes them very steady on their feet and hard to bring down, though they don't tend to be too stealthy or agile. Their skin is a light brown or deep tan with eyes, hair, and beards to match. Dwarves can live for more than four hundred years—some even breaking the millennium mark. They speak their own language, Dwarvish, and worship a pantheon of dwarf gods led by Moradin the Soul Forger.

GAUNTLGRYM

The legendary subterranean dwarf hold of Gauntlgrym was built by the ancient dwarves of Delzoun for the humans of Illusk. Though once home to thousands of humans and dwarves, its place in the world has slipped from the memory of even the oldest dwarf, and no records of its exact location exist, but many dwarves (including Bruenor Battlehammer) still tell tales of its mighty halls and mightier treasures. If it still exists at all, it's surely now home to the vile dregs of the Underdark, the creeping, crawling, malevolent things that are always on the hunt for a dark corner in which to hide—oblivious to or contemptuous of the grand history that still haunts its silent halls.

REGIS

Regis hung his head and could not answer. Entreri's words rang true enough. His friends were coming into dangers they could not imagine, and all for his sake, all because of errors he had made before he had ever met them.

—*The Halfling's Gem*

The nimble-fingered Regis is a bit less than three feet of solid halfling, from the top of his head of curly brown hair to his fur-topped bare feet. His belly is ample, and his legs are short. With a cherubic, dimpled face, Regis easily can be mistaken for a portly human child, but behind that childlike facade is a well-traveled, smart, and wily adult. That cuddly appearance is disturbed only by two missing fingers—taken from him by his most hated enemy, the assassin Artemis Entreri.

Regis hails from the desert city of Calimport, far to the south of his current home in Mithral Hall. There he grew up on the streets, making his living by his wits and those aforementioned nimble fingers. He rose up the ranks of the cutpurses to take a place in the thieves' guild run by the notorious Pasha Pook. But it didn't take long for Regis to get himself into trouble, stealing a collection of precious gems from Pook. He quickly found himself on the run—and didn't stop until he got all the way to Icewind Dale.

There he spends some time in Lonelywood and fancies himself the only halfling within hundreds of miles of that frontier town. With a mix of his natural charm and a certain enchanted ruby pendant, Regis comes to represent Lonelywood on the council of Ten-Towns, where he trades with Bryn Shander. Though respected and well liked by the people of Ten-Towns—even being honored with the title of First Citizen—Regis is known to pine for his days on the hot, crowded, and exciting streets of Calimport. Still, he considers Ten-Towns and Icewind Dale his true home now and only reluctantly stays at Mithral Hall with his boon companions Bruenor and Drizzt. No matter where he is, he keeps tabs on the ins and outs of Ten-Towns.

Called "Rumblebelly" by his friend Bruenor Battlehammer, for reasons that should be obvious, Regis is a typical halfling in more than appearance. He never misses a meal—at least, not without complaining about it—and is easily tempted by comfort, sweets, and good company. Though a loyal friend, not everyone is sure about Regis's motives, since many of his friends have fallen "victim" to his ruby pendant and not always for their own good.

His upbringing as a street thief has left him a little greedy, a little too easy to tempt into some bad ideas, and a little too quick to brush off feelings like guilt and remorse. Still, he works harder than the average halfling and, taken in balance, he's led a productive and busy life. Though he complains incessantly before, during, and after any voyage, he's quite well traveled and has even spent a while aboard ships, the form of travel he likes the least—maybe even less than the average water-wary halfling does.

Regis dislikes combat and can be quite creative in the means he employs to avoid a fight. If he has to, he can and will sneak up on the back of a fight and wield his mace in hand-to-hand combat—all the while blaming his reckless friends for getting him into such a mess.

Regis's skills may be lacking in combat, but he's got other redeeming qualities. He's a scrimshander of remarkable talent and a master storyteller. His snore is as loud as his gurgling belly, and the reason he hates boats? He can't swim.

Besides the magical mace that was given to him by Bruenor, Regis wears fine armor forged by Buster Bracer, and his jeweled belt is a throwback to his days as a thief. When he was the guildmaster of his own thieves' guild in Calimport, he wore a tunic embroidered with a thousand gemstones. But still his most prized possession is his ruby pendant.

Regis is a true survivor, and though he can often be heard complaining about the details, in the bigger picture he's undeniably charming and steadfast, moving forward at his friends' sides (though maybe just a step or two back), no matter how bleak the outcome may look.

THE RUBY PENDANT

Regis's most prized possession is a ruby pendant that he stole from Pasha Pook. Pook used the ruby's magical properties to climb the ranks of Calimport's underworld—and even came to depend on it—so he was not at all pleased when Regis made off with it.

The halfling wears the ruby pendant on a gold chain around his neck, and he doesn't hesitate to use its hypnotic powers when he sees fit. When he holds it up to the gaze of others, anyone but those with the most steadfast of wills is drawn into the myriad reflections on the gem's expertly cut surface. The images and the motion of the ruby bring about a deep sense of peace and well-being and leave the victim's mind open to suggestion.

These suggestions are so strong, so difficult to resist, that victims can even be convinced to do themselves harm. They're also so lasting that suggestions can be implanted in a victim's mind for days, tendays, even years before being triggered at a specified time or circumstance.

The downside is that those under the ruby's influence rarely perform at their best, and when the effect finally does wear off, they often know they've been manipulated and are none too happy with Regis!

SCRIMSHAW

The art of carving into bone and ivory, scrimshaw has been practiced by northern barbarian tribes and by the more civilized folk of Icewind Dale from time immemorial. Carvings tend to have nautical or hunting themes, the images etched into ivory using picks or knives. The etchings are then rubbed with ink to make the images stand out on the polished white of the bone or tusk. Scrimshaw is a popular export from Icewind Dale to points south, and Regis is considered perhaps the greatest scrimshander in Ten-Towns. He often carves scenes into the skulls of the knucklehead trout native to the cold lakes of Icewind Dale.

HALFLINGS

Closely related to humans, the halflings are small folk who are as likely to be thieves and pickpockets as they are to be hardworking tradesmen and responsible citizens. It's rare to find a halfling taller than three feet, and their propensity to laugh and lay about makes it easy for the taller races to dismiss them as silly, weak, or childlike, but halflings are as smart as any human and often use that intelligence for personal gain. Though they have a language of their own, it's very rarely heard. Most halflings tend to stick to the Common Tongue, leading some to believe their language is some kind of a secret. Though there is a halfling realm far in the southeastern reaches of Faerûn called Luiren, most halflings prefer to live in small, scattered communities of their own or to intermingle with humans in towns and cities.

ARTEMIS ENTRERI

When a pasha hired Artemis Entreri to kill a man, that man was soon dead. Without exception. And despite the many enemies he had obviously made, the assassin had been able to walk the streets of Calimport openly, not from shadow to shadow, in all confidence that none would be bold enough to act against him.

—*The Silent Blade*

Artemis Entreri is a grim-faced man with angular features—a strong jawline and high cheekbones. His dark gray eyes are so hard they can appear almost lifeless—cold and penetrating. The assassin's slender frame moves with a quick, precise confidence. His cloak is as black as his straight, short hair and covers a simple leather jerkin.

Entreri is more than merely a killer for hire; he is widely believed to be the finest assassin in all the Realms. He has never failed to track down and dispatch anyone he was sent to kill, even if he has to range thousands of miles from his home city of Calimport on the far southwestern coast of Faerûn.

In Calimport, Entreri has served as Pasha Pook's most favored assassin and has become a legend in that crowded city's underworld. Before coming into the employ of Pasha Pook, Entreri was made a lieutenant in the Basadoni Guild at the tender age of fourteen—if the likes of Artemis Entreri could ever have been described as "tender." After leaving Pook's guild, Entreri spends time in the dark elf city of Menzoberranzan at the side of his unlikely compatriot Jarlaxle Baenre of the drow mercenary company Bregan D'aerthe. But that stay is only temporary (Entreri doesn't like spiders), and the assassin continues to maintain a network of contacts, patrons, and informers in Calimport.

But it's Artemis Entreri's hatred of one particular dark elf, the renegade Drizzt, that has become the central obsession of his life. It's difficult to say what a man like Entreri might have to prove, but there's no doubt he means to prove it—at least to himself—by taking the life of Drizzt Do'Urden.

Is it something that happened to him as a child? Was he born without a conscience? Is he devoid of any moral compass? Or perhaps it is simply the demands of his unique profession that have made Artemis Entreri the cold, callous, grim, and ruthless man he's become. No one will ever know for sure, because Artemis Entreri will never let anyone close enough to him to find out.

The assassin considers emotion a weakness and relies on his strong will, his cautious and thorough planning, and the aura of fear he surrounds himself with to keep him alive and to bring death to his enemies. He always prepares for the worst eventuality, so he is rarely if ever surprised, even if things go horribly wrong. Like most assassins, Entreri works alone and has no patience for anyone who intrudes on his secretive life. Artemis Entreri is so uninterested in politics and relationships that he has never married and has avoided taking a leadership position in any guild of assassins or thieves. Like a rogue shark, he works alone.

His favored weapon is an enchanted dagger with an emerald-encrusted hilt, and his skill with the weapon is virtually unmatched. Like his sworn enemy, Drizzt, he also favors a two-handed fighting style, with his dagger in one hand and a heavy-bladed saber in the other. His skills match Drizzt's, but he lacks the unusual dark elf's passion and sense of right and wrong.

Entreri has magically enhanced darkvision that causes his eyes to glow a beastly red. He has all the skills of a sneak thief and can move with feline grace and silence. During his short time in Menzoberranzan, he picked up some of the silent sign language of the drow. And that's no easy feat. The dark elves' silent speech is far more complex and subtle than any human thieves' guild's simple handcant.

Artemis Entreri has never hesitated to kill but is a keen observer and has a strong instinct for self-preservation, so he knows when to talk his way out of a jam and when to fight his way out.

ENTRERI'S DAGGER

Truly a weapon of the vilest evil, this jewel-encrusted dagger steals the life-force from its victim and transfers that energy to the wielder. For every wound he inflicts with this vampiric blade, Artemis Entreri grows stronger. Victims are wracked with body-twisting convulsions and are made to suffer through the experience of feeling their very life essences drawn from them.

The dagger was crafted by the Thayan necromancer Thivris Ull in the Year of the Haunted Crew (959 DR) and was stolen less than a tenday later by his own apprentice, who fled back to his ancestral home in Calimport. It came into Entreri's possession centuries later when the assassin killed the apprentice's great-great-grandson on the orders of Pasha Pook.

JARLAXLE

Jarlaxle shifted to the side and winced as his weight came upon his recently wounded leg. Triel Baenre herself, the matron mistress of Arach-Tinilith, had tended the wound, but Jarlaxle suspected that the wicked priestess had purposely left the job unfinished, had left a bit of the pain to remind the mercenary of his failure in recapturing the renegade Drizzt Do'Urden.

—*Starless Night*

Jarlaxle Baenre, son of the matron mother of the First House, is the leader of the mercenary company Bregan D'aerthe and one of the most powerful and influential males in the matriarchal City of Spiders.

On the outside, Jarlaxle appears to be a handsome, flamboyant dandy—unusual enough among the dark elves—but his outrageous appearance is a carefully crafted decoy hiding a pragmatic, intelligent, and observant leader. Even his cleanly shaved head gives him a tactical advantage—an opponent can't grab him by the hair. His wild clothing and jewelry carry a wide array of enchantments both offensive and defensive in nature. Jarlaxle walks with a limp from an injury that has never completely healed.

Like many drow males, Jarlaxle was trained in combat at Melee-Magthere, where he excelled in the less direct forms of physical combat. He was recognized early on as a brilliant strategist and tactician, but he always preferred the stealthy dagger of an assassin to the flashing swords of his fellow students.

Jarlaxle went on to found the mercenary company Bregan D'aerthe, which provides soldiers, spies, and scouts for anyone with sufficient coin. He maintains close ties to the House of his birth but fiercely guards his independence.

Unlike the nobles of the ruling Houses, Jarlaxle is more egalitarian in his dealings with non-drow and has close associates among humans, illithids, svirfneblin—anyone or anything he thinks will be a valuable ally or a ready source of gold or information.

For centuries he's felt something was wrong in the city of his birth and rejects what he sees as an egocentric view that everything in Menzoberranzan is a direct result of the will of Lolth. He has seen behind the curtain of the matron mothers' various plots and schemes a few too many times and has survived for centuries thanks to a healthy cynicism.

Truly chaotic in nature, Jarlaxle always keeps his opponents and friends alike guessing. He can be funny one moment and dire the next. Cagey, sarcastic, insightful, and impossible to pin down, he's got a curious and almost joyful approach to his work with Bregan D'aerthe and to his position in the City of Spiders—a place he'd just as soon sell out or abandon than protect.

He can't resist irony—the more bitter the irony, the wider he grins—and is a sucker for exotic magic. All of these qualities tend to work against him among the matron mothers, who find him arrogant and unpredictable.

Among his many skills is a facility for languages. He can speak fluently in the Common Tongue of the World Above, in the rough language of the svirfneblin, and in the Abyssal speech of the Lower Planes.

Whatever language he's speaking, chances are he's lying—or is he?

A FEW OF JARLAXLE'S MAGIC ITEMS

It's possible that Jarlaxle himself doesn't know how many magic items he's collected over the years, and there are only a few he's seen with more than once or twice.

Perhaps his favorite is the wide-brimmed purple hat with its long and flamboyant diatryma feather. More than a fashion accessory, the hat allows Jarlaxle to change his physical features, disguising himself as nearly any sort of humanoid. The eye patch he wears—which eye it covers is ruled by some chaotic whim known only to Jarlaxle—protects him from spells that could reveal his thoughts.

His boots allow him to choose how quietly or how loudly he moves across any surface, and he carries a whistle that can be heard only by members of his band. Even the jewelry he wears will jingle when he wants it to or lay perfectly silent if he doesn't want to be heard.

BREGAN D'AERTHE

Bregan D'aerthe is a mercenary society that provides warriors, spies, and scouts to the highest bidder—and sometimes to all bidders. It's a rare conflict in and around Menzoberranzan that doesn't involve them in one way or another. There are some one-hundred-and-fifty members of the company, both drow and goblinoid.

Bregan D'aerthe is crewed mainly by rogue male drow drawn from the lower ranks of the major Houses and from the tattered remnants of destroyed Houses. Male dark elves aren't highly prized, and when a House is disbanded, the male drow have little hope of finding a new House to become a part of. But Jarlaxle is always looking for another capable warrior, wizard, or tracker.

DROW OF MENZOBERRANZAN

HOUSE BAENRE

YVONNEL BAENRE

Matron Mother Yvonnel Baenre is the powerful matriarch of the First House of Menzoberranzan and the closest thing the City of Spiders has ever had to a queen. In Menzoberranzan, the priestesses of Lolth rule with an iron fist and are organized in a series of noble Houses, ranked by the sheer power they possess and their unrelenting willingness to wield it. House Baenre commands the loyalty of more of the larger Houses than any other and also enjoys very close ties to the Academy and to the mercenary company Bregan D'aerthe.

Matron Mother Baenre's spies are everywhere, and she's not the least bit hesitant to employ non-drow, including illithids and even humans, to forward her twisted schemes. Of her twenty children, fifteen are high priestesses, so her tendrils reach deep into the clergy of the Spider Queen.

Older than any other drow known, Matron Mother Baenre was born in the Year of the Ill-Timed Truth (-685 DR) and lives for two-thousand-forty-three years before she finally falls to Bruenor Battlehammer's many-notched axe.

She is succeeded by her eldest daughter, Triel.

GROMPH BAENRE

The most powerful wizard in the City of Spiders, Matron Mother Baenre's eldest son, Gromph, is the Archmage of Menzoberranzan, Master of Sorcere, and the highest-ranking male drow in the city. The archmage has made sure that while the female drow both hold the reigns of power and control the clergy of Lolth, the arcane arts are in the hands of male drow, an advantage that will only show its true depths many years hence.

Though the position includes some ceremonial duties, like maintaining Narbondel, Menzoberranzan's great stalagmite "clock," Gromph is truly in a position of power. He's a formidable spellcaster and has access to Sorcere's impressive storehouse of magical items and artifacts. He's held the position of archmage longer than any drow before him, and he doesn't seem to be going anywhere soon.

Born in the Year of Many Floods (670 DR), he's lived for some seven centuries, but thanks to a magical brooch, he appears perpetually young. This arrogant, surly, and temperamental wizard remains loyal to his mother but isn't above the occasional petty dispute. He's been at odds with his sister Quenthel for decades and has thrown in his lot with Triel, whom he's supported as the heir to the House Baenre throne— an heir he's convinced he can manipulate to his own ends.

BERG'INYON BAENRE

The youngest son of the matron mother, Berg'inyon is the weapons master of House Baenre, the House's principal military leader, and its most skilled warrior. He trained at Melee-Magthere alongside Drizzt Do'Urden, to whom Berg'inyon always came in second, even though his fighting arm is strong and his style fluid and deadly. Berg'inyon has never forgiven Drizzt for outclassing him, and that hatred still runs deep.

He worked his way up through the ranks of the House Baenre lizard riders and can still be found leading his troops from astride one of those mighty beasts. Berg'inyon wields a death lance, a weapon that turns those it kills into undead.

One of his duties as weapons master is to coordinate his mother's security, and he was chosen for the post for his fierce loyalty to her. His brother Dantrag may be the better fighter, and his brother Gromph holds decidedly more political power, but neither of them were ever as close to their powerful mother as he is.

QUENTHEL BAENRE

After the death of Matron Mother Baenre, Quenthel is the highest-ranking priestess of Lolth in Menzoberranzan. Said to be favored by the Queen of the Demonweb Pits, Quenthel set her sights on the title of Mistress Mother of Arach-Tinilith early on, and she has risen to the rank of high priestess faster than any before her.

The only one left in her way is her sister Triel, and it is this rivalry that is at the root of a burning animosity between the two sisters. Quenthel's contempt for the arcane arts also draws the ire of her powerful brother Gromph until she is killed by the renegade Drizzt Do'Urden.

But that isn't the last Menzoberranzan will see of Quenthel Baenre. Years later she'll be brought back from the dead by Lolth herself, and even Triel and Gromph can't prevent her from finally seizing the post she always coveted: Mistress Mother of Arach-Tinilith.

TRIEL BAENRE

Triel rises to the lofty post of Mistress Mother of Arach-Tinilith before stepping into the position of matron mother when Yvonnel is killed by Bruenor.

She shares her brother Gromph's burning ambition—and hatred of their sister Quenthel—but doesn't share his crafty, calm intelligence. Triel is a less accomplished politician, making decisions based on emotion rather than through strategic thinking.

She is smart enough, however, to know that once she's attained the position of matron mother, she'll be able to groom her own children for positions of power throughout Menzoberranzan. She slips into the role of leader easily enough, carrying herself with a grace and arrogant dignity that belies her incendiary temper.

BLADEN'KERST BAENRE

The second oldest daughter of Matron Mother Baenre, Bladen'Kerst might have been assigned a minor House of her own, but she is so cruel and difficult to control that she's been held back at House Baenre, where she's been put in charge of torturing captives. Lacking even the cold civility of the drow, Bladen'Kerst revels in causing pain. She's particularly contemptuous of male drow, whom she sees merely as test subjects for her latest techniques for inflicting agony.

She meets her end when Gandalug Battlehammer strangles her with her own whip.

VENDES BAENRE

Another daughter of Matron Mother Baenre, Vendes is sadistic and wicked. Like her sister Bladen'Kerst, Vendes enjoys the art of torture and goes about her assignments with a grim relish that has earned her the nickname Duk-Tak, from the drow word for "unholy executioner." Some of the few monuments to adorn the City of Spiders are the forms of drow she's turned into ebony statues.

Vendes is eventually killed by Drizzt, bringing her reign of terror to an end—but ultimately just leaving the torture chamber door open to another mistress. There is no shortage of vicious, blood-thirsty drow in Menzoberranzan.

SOS'UMPTU BAENRE

Sos'Umptu may be her mother's greatest disappointment and surely is the least ambitious priestess of her House, if not in all of Menzoberranzan. A mid-ranked cleric, she is the caretaker of the Baenre chapel, a complex she rarely leaves. Sos'Umptu seems content to serve her mother and her goddess and leaves herself out of the constant political machinations of her siblings.

She spends most of her time slowly creating a golem in the form of a jeweled spider to guard the Baenre chapel.

DANTRAG BAENRE

Once the weapons master of House Baenre, Dantrag is a better fighter than his brother Berg'inyon but still no match for Drizzt. When the renegade from House Do'Urden finally kills him, Dantrag's favorite sword, the sentient and malignant blade Khazid'hea, falls into the hands of a human woman, and the bracers that gave him preternatural speed in combat are taken by Drizzt himself.

House Do'Urden

Malice Do'Urden

Malice Do'Urden is the matriarch of House Do'Urden and Drizzt's mother. She is a high-ranking priestess of Lolth, who is also a skilled alchemist capable of mixing various potions, elixirs, and salves. Her ability to bind a spirit-wraith, a process she performed on one of her former lovers—Drizzt's father, Zaknafein—frightens even the other drow priestesses around her.

She lives for five centuries in the unforgiving City of Spiders, relying on cunning and treachery to see her through. As cruel and ambitious as any matron mother of Menzoberranzan, Malice's greed eventually gets the better of her, and House Do'Urden falls with its matriarch in the Year of the Lion (1340 DR).

Zaknafein Do'Urden

Once the finest weapons master in Menzoberranzan, Zaknafein of House Do'Urden is also Drizzt's father. Though in his nearly four centuries of life, Zaknafein defeats everything from demons to elementals, he likes to kill drow most of all, especially priestesses of Lolth. That sacrilege—among others—leads to his eventual sacrifice at the hands of Matron Malice. But before he meets his doom, he is able to help his son escape the clutches of the vile matriarchy of the City of Spiders.

Zaknafein prefers the two-sword style of Melee-Magthere, the warriors' academy of Menzoberranzan, and he passes that style on to his son. Only after nearly killing Drizzt in single combat does Zaknafein learn that his son shares his distaste for dark elf customs. Like Drizzt, Zaknafein considers himself a drow only by the color of his skin.

DININ DO'URDEN

Dinin is born the second son of Malice Baenre but kills his older brother Nalfein the moment he has an opportunity and rises in the ranks to Elderboy. That particular murder is well-timed for Drizzt, who is to be sacrificed as the third son but moves up to Secondboy with Nalfein's premature demise.

A skilled fighter, Dinin rises in the ranks of Melee-Magthere to become a Master of the Academy. Not long after killing Nalfein, Dinin joins Jarlaxle's Bregan D'aerthe and so impresses the mercenary leader that Jarlaxle takes to calling him *Khal'abbil*, "my trusted friend."

Though Jarlaxle might trust him, Dinin's own sister Vierna never really does, and she eventually turns him into one of the hideous half-drow, half-spider monstrosities known as a drider. She takes control of his broken mind and spirit to ride him like some hellish mount.

VIERNA DO'URDEN

The second daughter of Malice Do'Urden, Vierna was expected to slink into the background, but she has ambitions of her own. Her mother charges her with the upbringing of her brother Drizzt when the boy is but a toddler, and for the first five years of his life, Vierna instills in her brother the rigorous evil of the dark elf matriarchy. Only much later does she become a high priestess and set her sights on her mother's throne. Equally at home in the wild Underdark as on the streets and in the mansions of Menzoberranzan, Vierna eventually finds herself the last hope for her doomed House. She becomes so accomplished a priestess that she's able to mutate her brother Dinin into a drider, all the better to hunt down and sacrifice her only other surviving brother, Drizzt.

NALFEIN DO'URDEN

Nalfein is sent to study magic at Sorcere, where he shows considerable talent. He then goes on to serve as the House wizard for his mother but isn't terribly well liked by his siblings—who don't tend to like anyone, anyway.

Perhaps his greatest accomplishment, other than being the first-born male of House Do'Urden, is allowing himself to be killed by his younger brother Dinin, inadvertently sparing the infant Drizzt's life.

BRIZA DO'URDEN

Malice's eldest daughter is Briza, a priestess of Lolth most notable
for her stocky and intimidating physical presence. But Briza isn't
only physically intimidating. She is a tough and angry sort, with a
sharp tongue that gets her in trouble with her superiors and strikes
fear into those of lesser rank. Briza is always the first to punish one
of her brothers or anyone else unfortunate enough to cross her.

MAYA DO'URDEN

Maya Do'Urden is the youngest of Matron Mother Malice's
three daughters and never quite manages to come into her own.
Though she is a slender girl, she possesses surprising strength
and shares her mother's darker tendencies.

It is Maya who senses the death of Nalfein and stops—at the
very last moment—the sacrificial murder of the infant Drizzt.

RIZZEN DO'URDEN

Rizzen becomes the patron of House Do'Urden after Malice strips Zaknafein of that
rank. The title is largely, if not entirely, ceremonial, and Rizzen takes his orders from
Briza as often as from Malice. A warrior and former student of Zaknafein's, Rizzen
also possesses limited wizardly abilities—enough to make him useful to Malice and
irritating to Briza, who goes as far as to beat him with her snake-headed whip.

He enjoys rubbing Zaknafein's face in the fact that he's taken his former master's
position as patron, but Zaknafein remains unfazed. The first patron of House
Do'Urden finally gets his revenge, though, when Zaknafein, then a spirit-wraith,
kills his successor.

The Matron Mothers

Mez'Barris Armgo

The matron mother of the powerful Second House of Menzoberranzan, House Barrison Del'Armgo, Mez'Barris is most unusual among the matron mothers for her love of single combat. She's the only sitting matron mother who will actually lead her troops into melee. Big even by drow female standards, Mez'Barris is a fierce warrior who will employ any number of magic items, including gloves that endow her with great strength and a pair of enchanted maces she's named *Qu'lith* ("Blood") and *Qu'uente* ("Guts").

House Barrison Del'Armgo is one of the younger Houses in Menzoberranzan, but they fought their way to the second rank through centuries of challengers met and defeated. Both their warriors and their mages are considered the best in the City of Spiders, and the other Houses know better than to challenge Mez'Barris again. Choosing to stay above the political fray, Mez'Barris avoids close alliances with other Houses, surrounding herself with her five daughters and with her patron, Uthegental, one of Menzoberranzan's premiere weapons masters.

SiNafay Hun'ett

House Hun'ett has achieved the position of Fifth House in the City of Spiders, but its matron mother holds more ambition in her tiny frame than is typical, even for her power-mad ilk. Determined to drag her House forward in the rankings, SiNafay targets House Do'Urden for destruction, to her ultimate loss. She is a high priestess as loyal to the Spider Queen as any, and she uses the idea that House Do'Urden has fallen from Lolth's favor against them. But still she is not able to prevent the eventual destruction of House Hun'ett. House Q'Xorlarrin rises to replace House Hun'ett as Fifth House.

K'YORL ODRAN

Matron Mother K'yorl Odran of House Oblodra, the Third House of Menzoberranzan, appears to be the most unassuming, least threatening of the matron mothers, but that pastoral front hides a dangerous secret. K'yorl is a psionicist of remarkable talent, and she relies on those powers of the mind—not armor, weapons, or even bodyguards—to protect her from her enemies, and she has many enemies indeed, including House Baenre.

Secretive but at the same time unsubtle, her infamous grin tells anyone paying attention that she's lying and doesn't care who knows it. K'yorl is the most despised of Menzoberranzan's matron mothers.

GHENNI'TIROTH TLABBAR

The priestesses of the Fourth House, Faen Tlabbar, are the most fanatical in Menzoberranzan and have been favored by Lolth with the ability to create new spells in the Spider Queen's name. Ghenni'tiroth has been House Faen Tlabbar's matron mother for more than three centuries but was not born into that role. She is a refugee from Zaereth'uul, a minor House that was destroyed in the Year of the Dreamforging (1033 DR).

Even in the theocratic matriarchy of Menzoberranzan, the Faen Tlabbar priestesses are feared for the intensity of their worship of Lolth, and that fanaticism has kept the House in the higher ranks for more than six centuries. It also doesn't hurt that Ghenni'tiroth maintains close ties to both House Baenre and House Xorlarrin.

ZEERITH Q'XORLARRIN

The paranoid and reclusive Fifth House is based in the Spelltower Xorlarrin, a tall and graceful tower that rises majestically above the Qu'ellarz'orl plateau. Matron Mother Zeerith leads House Xorlarrin with a lighter hand than any of her counterparts, actively seeking opinions and input even from the male drow of her House. Xorlarrin males are bred for their magic ability, and infants who show no signs of an inclination toward the Art are sacrificed. This has given House Xorlarrin a solid reputation as one of the most magically gifted—and therefore dangerous—of the noble Houses of Menzoberranzan. Zeerith is so secretive that she insists the nobles of her House wear masks whenever they venture out onto the streets of Menzoberranzan.

AURO'POL DYRR

Though rumor has it that the true power behind Agrach Dyrr, the Sixth House of Menzoberranzan, is actually the lichdrow Dyrr, Matron Mother Auro'pol is a prominent figure in the city and a high priestess not to be trifled with. Agrach Dyrr is among the oldest Houses and one of the most aggressive. Many minor Houses have fallen victim to Auro'pol in her more than four hundred years as matron mother. She maintains a close alliance with the First House, though there is no love lost between Gromph Baenre and the lichdrow Dyrr.

MIZ'RI MIZZRYM

The otherwise unassuming Seventh House makes its home in a stalactite hanging from the ceiling of the great cavern of Menzoberranzan. Matron Mother Miz'ri has managed to form alliances with all of the other ruling Houses of Menzoberranzan, which keeps her House largely out of trouble and free to concentrate on commerce. Well-known as treacherous and cunning negotiators, House Mizzrym commands a vast fortune, allowing Miz'ri to employ mercenaries to protect her House. Her skill at cutting the best deal also has indebted many of the other Houses to Mizzrym interests.

A Rogues' Gallery
of the City of Spiders

"It is the drow way," Drizzt said calmly, matter-of-factly, trying to impart the dark elves' casual attitude toward murder. "There is a strict structure of rank in Menzoberranzan. To climb it, to attain a higher rank, whether as an individual or a family, you simply eliminate those above you."

—*Sojourn*

Masoj Hun'ett

The first dark elf killed by Drizzt Do'Urden, Masoj Hun'ett is an apprentice wizard, finishing thirty years of training at Sorcere. Masoj is caught up in the vile politics of the City of Spiders and throws in his lot with his family against House Do'Urden. When his alliance with the Faceless One disintegrates, he kills the disfigured mage and takes from him a small onyx figurine—the figurine of wondrous power that calls Guenhwyvar.

Though fond of his heavy crossbow, Masoj is a gifted spellcaster and relies on his magic to get ahead. Part of his duties at Sorcere is to train the young Drizzt in the ways of magic, but Drizzt impresses him far more as a warrior than as a wizard. Masoj enjoys the moments leading up to all-out war, the maneuvering and backstabbing, but in the end, his lack of experience is his undoing.

The Faceless One

The Faceless One is so named because of the hideous burns that erased his features, replacing them with a ghoulish mask of pale white tissue and sickly green slime. Before that fateful experiment destroyed his face, he was Gelroos Hun'ett, a master of Sorcere. He still seeks out spells that will restore his ravaged face and is willing to sell his own powerful magic for the slimmest hope of restoration.

UTHEGENTAL

Uthegental is the proud and mighty weapons master and patron of House Barrison Del'Armgo. Considered one of the most powerful warriors in the City of Spiders, what Uthegental lacks in grace and agility, he makes up for in sheer strength and brutality. In battle he usually allows his opponent to draw first blood, letting himself be wounded just enough to bring on a berserk frenzy. He then tears his opponent to pieces and eats him, so feral does he become.

Despite this grotesque practice—or perhaps because of it—he's the consort of many of the House Barrison Del'Armgo females, not just their matron mother.

From left to right: Uthegental, Kimmuriel, Hatch'net, Rai'gy

KIMMURIEL OBLODRA

Kimmuriel is one of the few survivors of House Oblodra, which was pulled into the Clawrift and obliterated by House Baenre. He goes to work, as Houseless males are wont to do, for Jarlaxle's Bregan D'aerthe, where he proves his worth with the uncanny powers of his mind. Kimmuriel is a talented and dangerous psionicist. His dimension doors allow Jarlaxle and his agents to move across long distances with a single step, and when employed as an assassin, Kimmuriel proves to be as creative as he is cruel.

Devoted to the psychic arts, Kimmuriel has an arrogant dislike for traditional arcane magic but is pragmatic enough to work with wizards like Rai'gy or to use the occasional magic item. He has contacts among the illithids that also prove valuable to Bregan D'aerthe.

HATCH'NET

Hatch'net has been the Loremaster of Melee-Magthere for over two hundred years. He holds court over his students in an oval lecture hall that helps his booming voice carry to the ears of his eager pupils. His manner of speaking is hypnotic, and the tales he tells of the tragic history of the dark elf race are so compelling that his students are not allowed to bring weapons into the chamber lest they get carried away with the rage his lessons instill in them. Hatch'net tells them of the fall of the drow and the promise that they will one day rise against their surface elf oppressors.

He then goes on to preside over the grand melee and leads his students on their first patrol. Many a young drow has had his worldview shaped by Master Hatch'net.

RAI'GY BONDALEK

Rai'gy is a wizard-priest from the drow city of Ched Nasad, who comes to Menzoberranzan to work as a spy for Bregan D'aerthe when House Bondalek is stripped of its status and absorbed by Houses Seulakk, K'zhaazz, and Melarn. He's become one of Jarlaxle's trusted lieutenants, prized for his multifaceted talents in spellcasting. Not a terribly pleasant sort, Rai'gy likes to keep others off balance, bending them to his timetable as a way of exerting subtle control over them.

He employs an imp named Druzil as his familiar. This minor fiend has a poisoned barb at the end of its tail and flies on leathery wings. Imps serve as counselors and spies for the devils of the Nine Hells—or the occasional drow wizard. They possess inherent magical abilities that allow them to change their shape at will, regenerate wounds, and even commune with higher powers.

KHAREESA H'KAR

Khareesa is a slaver who provides goblins and orcs for the farms on the Isle of Rothé. As passionate as she is beautiful, she makes the mistake of striking up a conversation with Drizzt, though she has no idea at first who he is, on one of his rare trips back to the city of his birth. She is soon killed by agents of Bregan D'aerthe.

Sometimes, life and death in Menzoberranzan hangs on just a little luck.

DWELLERS IN THE UNDERDARK

Malice composed herself quickly. Mind flayers were not unknown in Menzoberranzan, and rumors said that one had befriended Matron Baenre. These creatures, though, more intelligent and more evil than even the drow, almost always inspired shudders of revulsion.

—Homeland

CLACKER

Clacker started his life as a pech, one of the unassuming and reclusive races of goodly humanoids that live deep in the earth, working the stone in search of precious metals and gems. Pech have innate magical abilities that help make them one with the stone that surrounds them, and though small and seemingly primitive, they are intelligent and wise in the ways of the Underdark.

Clacker is transformed into a towering hook horror by the wizard Brister Fendlestick, but kills the wizard before he can be changed back. Over time he begins to lose touch with his pech self and more and more becomes a hook horror in spirit as well as form.

Hook horrors are nine-foot-tall monstrosities that appear to be part bird and part insect. Though intelligent, hook horrors are primitive tribal hunters that jealously guard their subterranean hunting grounds. They get their names from the massive hooked appendages they have in place of hands.

Zaknafein kills Clacker before he has a chance to return to his true form, a tragedy Drizzt holds with him forever.

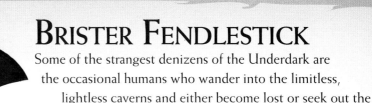

BRISTER FENDLESTICK

Some of the strangest denizens of the Underdark are the occasional humans who wander into the limitless, lightless caverns and either become lost or seek out the reclusive life of a hermit. There's no way to know what first brought the human wizard Brister Fendlestick down into the Underdark, but he has found a way to survive there, living in a magical tower he can shrink down and carry in one of his voluminous extradimensional pockets.

Paranoid and obviously quite mad, Brister is quick to lash out at anyone who intrudes on his studies, catches him filling buckets from an underground stream, happens upon his iron tower, or otherwise crosses his path.

But when he turns one innocent pech into a hook horror, he makes his final error.

EL-VIDDENVELP

Also known as Methil, this hideous illithid lives in the House Baenre stronghold and has been a close advisor of the First House's matron mother for many years. Like all of its kind, El-Viddenvelp is a powerful psionicist that hungers for the thoughts of other sentient beings. It is capable of seeing deep into the thoughts of anyone it comes in contact with, giving Matron Mother Baenre access into her enemies' most closely guarded secrets.

It's badly wounded by Catti-brie and Regis, and though it's able to escape, its own brain begins to leak out of its rubbery skull. There have been occasional, unconfirmed sightings ever since of a mad, drooling illithid stalking the caverns around Menzoberranzan, muttering incoherently and from time to time feasting on the simple brains of escaped kobold slaves.

THE DEEP GNOMES OF BLINGDENSTONE

BELWAR DISSENGULP

Belwar Dissengulp is the Most Honored Burrow-Warden of the svirfneblin city of Blingdenstone. He lost his hands to Dinin Do'Urden but made the best of a bad situation by having them replaced with the tools of the deep gnomes' trade: an enchanted hammer and pick. When he calls out, *"Bivrip!"* the "hands" allow him to burrow through solid stone at a phenomenal rate.

Belwar is a smart and experienced digger who knows the ins and outs of life in the Underdark. Though he knows better than to befriend a drow, he recognizes some quality in Drizzt, and the two become close friends. Still, he almost continually fears a drow invasion of his home and always stands ready to protect it.

He speaks the language of his people, as well as the languages of the drow and goblins, in a deep, resonating voice unusual for his kind. Around his neck he wears a summoning stone that lets him call upon the services of an earth elemental.

Born in the Year of the Molten Man (1151 DR), he's almost two hundred years old.

KING SCHNICKTICK

King Schnicktick is the steady-handed ruler of Blingdenstone. Much of his time is spent preparing for what he believes is an inevitable drow invasion of his city. He is so convinced of its imminence that after five days of prayer, he orders the city evacuated. He's surprised, though pleasantly, by the number of his citizens who are brave enough to volunteer to scout the tunnels under Mithral Hall and root out the drow advance, but still the cautious king limits the number to three hundred.

FIRBLE

Firble is one of the councilors of Blingdenstone and has a secret relationship with Jarlaxle, who comes to him to trade information. Though Firble likes to be out in the Underdark, he has grown more and more suspicious and fearful of late—and with dark elves creeping around, he has a lot to be suspicious about. Firble can be impatient, and though he fears Jarlaxle, he is willing to press the mercenary for information, even if the dark elf presses back.

From left to right: *Belwar, King Schnicktick, Firble, Brickers, Krieger*

SVIRFNEBLIN

Standing no more than three-and-a-half feet tall, the svirfneblin, or deep gnomes, are industrious and civilized humanoids with spirits much larger than their frail-looking bodies would seem capable of holding. They live their lives surrounded by evil beings like drow and kuo-toa, so they are very, very careful with their trust. Over the millennia they've developed the ability to go unnoticed—not quite invisible, yet they seem to fade from view.

Svirfneblin are accomplished stonemasons, miners, and gemcutters, and their artistry is valued throughout the Underdark. Breaking from their natural tendency to hide themselves away, they're willing to trade with their neighbors but remain fearful and skittish around non-svirfneblin.

They don't look much like their surface-dwelling gnome cousins. Generations of life in the Underdark have taken their toll on them. Only female svirfneblin have any hair at all; male svirfneblin are universally bald. Though they favor well-made weapons from around the world, they're most typically armed with various picks, axes, and hammers—the tools of their trade.

Svirfneblin are fond of the saying, *magga cammara*, which means, "by the stones."

BURROW-WARDEN BRICKERS

Burrow-Warden Brickers leads mining expeditions out into the Underdark and never neglects to call on Belwar to join them. He's a strong and trusted leader who knows his way around the deepest caverns and speaks the languages of the dark elves and goblins, though he avoids contact with both. Brickers is famous among his kind for having discovered the Brickers Lode, a huge deposit of silver the deep gnomes of Blingdenstone have been mining since the Year of the Black Hound (1296 DR).

BURROW-WARDEN KRIEGER

Like Brickers, Burrow-Warden Krieger leads mining expeditions in the Underdark. Old and experienced, Krieger knows all the tricks and challenges the Underdark might throw at him. He has a highly tuned ability to sense irregularities in stone and almost hears it tell him its stories. His stone sense is even more highly developed than most svirfneblin.

SERVANTS OF EVIL

AKAR KESSELL

The self-proclaimed Tyrant of Icewind Dale first came to that windswept land as an overly ambitious apprentice mage. There he's manipulated into murdering his mentor, Morkai the Red, with the promise of a position in Luskan's Hosttower of the Arcane. But Kessell is a mediocre mage at best, that promise turns out to be a lie, and he finds himself abandoned in the frozen snowscape of Icewind Dale.

A mix of the very best and very worst luck brings him to Crenshinibon, which has come to Faerûn and seeks out someone it can corrupt—and Akar Kessell is manipulated again. But this time, the promises are kept, and with the help of the Crystal Shard, he gathers an army of humanoids and marches out into Icewind Dale a would-be conqueror.

Five years after finding the Crystal Shard, Kessell commands the allegiance of numerous humanoid tribes including the orcs of the Severed Tongue and some ten thousand goblins. He also commands a clan of ogres, several trolls, two-score verbeeg, and a group of frost giants led by Biggrin. Even the powerful balor Errtu serves as his general.

But Akar Kessell isn't nearly the leader he pretends to be, and even Crenshinibon's influence can't prevent him from making the rash mistakes of an ill-trained youth. Perverted by greed and evil, Akar Kessell meets his doom in an avalanche. His own plans for the conquest of Ten-Towns, and the blades of Drizzt Do'Urden, prove his undoing.

BIGGRIN

The frost giant Biggrin serves as the tactical commander of Akar Kessell's humanoid army and is accompanied by a group of verbeeg. His upper lip was torn off by a wolf, leaving him permanently scarred, which is how he got his name: Big-Grin. He's given a magic mirror that he can use to travel instantly from his lair on the slopes of Kelvin's Cairn to Akar Kessell's crystal fortress.

JUNGER

Like the rest of his primitive kind, the mountain giant Junger is an indiscriminate killer, charging headlong into battle against just about anything that passes him by. He is a little smarter than the average mountain giant, having some command of language, and he maintains a group of yetis to serve him as workers.

DEBERNEZAN

Ultimately killed by Regis, the traitor deBernezan sells his knowledge of Ten-Towns to betray the people who took him in as a merchant from the southern realm of Amn. He passes King Heafstaag's test of bravery, but only barely, and wets himself in the process. Still, he stands with the Tribe of the Bear in the service of Beorg when they attack Termalaine, and he meets his demise in an alley when the tide of battle turns against the barbarians.

RODDY MCGRISTLE

There is no shortage of beings, from dark elves to humans to creatures from the farthest depths of the Outer Planes, who have come to despise Drizzt Do'Urden, but few match the mad, almost frenzied hatred exhibited by the farmer-turned-bounty hunter Roddy McGristle. This crude, unpleasant man is a mediocre farmer but a reasonably skilled trapper, who spends more time in the mountains than tending to his fields. He's got a number of dogs, whose lives he values more than his neighbors', and he has an unlikely "friend" in the orc chief Graul. When he's sent to find the mysterious dark elf, Roddy's obsessive ways get the better of him, and though he tries to use Graul and his orcs then his own axe to kill Drizzt, all he manages to do is draw the ire of Bruenor Battlehammer, who eventually drives the temperamental bounty hunter from Icewind Dale.

Rumor has it that Roddy has relocated to a farmstead on the western edge of the Greenfields, where he breeds hunting dogs for the farmers and hunters of Greenest.

AGATHA

In life, Aeliantha of Aryvandaar was an elf sorceress of some talent, but when she died, her spirit lived on in the world as a banshee, a particularly terrifying undead creature whose keening wail is said to kill anyone unfortunate enough to hear it. Known as Agatha by the folk of the tiny village of Conyberry, near her forest lair in the Neverwinter Woods, she's become something of a local legend. The locals fear her but at the same time are convinced that she somehow protects them. She's collected a hoard of treasure over the centuries, including a certain magical mask that found its way into the hands of Drizzt Do'Urden.

GRAUL

Graul is the arrogant and violent chief of the orcs that inhabit the region around Dead Orc Pass. He plays the conquering hero with his own brutish people but shakes in his boots at the sight of a dark elf. Like all orcs he's mean and ill-tempered, greedy and slovenly, but capable of flashes of intelligence and good sense—neither of which he experiences when he decides to lead a raid on Mooshie's Grove.

Top: *Bloog*, Bottom (left to right): *Bathunk, Chogurugga, Bonko*

THE OGRES OF CLAN THUMP

The ogres of Clan Thump are led by the hearty female Chogurugga. They inhabit a system of caves overlooking Golden Cove on the far northern coast of the Sea of Swords, where they work closely with the pirate captain Sheila Kree. Chogurugga is the "brains" of the clan, but her mate, Bloog, is the muscle. At nearly fifteen feet, Bloog is bigger than the rest of the Clan Thump ogres, and some believe he has some mountain giant blood. Sheila Kree, in order to make him a more powerful ally, gives Bloog the stolen Aegis-fang to wield—at least for a little while.

Chogurugga and Bloog's son Bathunk doesn't seem to have inherited either his mother's brains or his father's brawn, but he's still a little bigger and a little stronger—and a little meaner—than the average ogre. And speaking of the average ogre, Bonko fits that bill nicely. He's as ill-mannered as he is slovenly, always ready to prey on the weak and bow to the strong.

BAELTIMAZIFAS

Baeltimazifas is a doppelganger, a strange humanoid creature that in its natural form appears almost as a blank slate. Like the rest of his malignant species, Baeltimazifas is able to assume the form and even the memories of anyone he encounters. He's then able to slip into their lives, fooling even his victim's closest friends. Though doppelgangers usually keep their own counsel and work toward their own monstrous agendas, Baeltimazifas has fallen under the thrall of a group of illithids.

PIRATES OF THE SEA OF SWORDS

SHEILA KREE

Sheila Kree is the captain of the pirate vessel *Bloody Keel*, which she renamed for her love of the classic pirate punishment, keelhauling. The ship was called *Leaping Lady* when she stole it and killed its merchant crew.

She maintains a hideout in the sea caves of Golden Cove on the far northern coast of the Sea of Swords, at the western tip of the Spine of the World. There she's found allies in Clan Thump, a tribe of ogres who also make their homes in the caves of Golden Cove.

Tough, unforgiving, and quick to beat her own crew, Sheila Kree is a pathological thief and killer. When she comes into possession of Aegis-fang, she uses the hammer to brand herself and her most trusted crewmembers—an enduring symbol of her stolen power.

CREEPS SHARKY

Creeps Sharky has sailed with pirates, merchant captains, whalers—anyone who'll have him—and he's been doing it for a long time. This crusty old sea dog counts lowlifes like Tee-a-nicknick and Morik the Rogue among his friends, and he has a burning dislike of Captain Deudermont. He once served as a crewman aboard the whaling vessel *Northwind Demon* and stayed on when her captain turned to piracy. It was *Sea Sprite* that sent *Northwind Demon* to the bottom of the Sea of Swords and sent Creeps to a stint in Baldur's Gate's dungeons.

CARRACKUS

Carrackus is a marine scrag, or saltwater troll, who serves with Captain Pinochet. Like their land-bound cousins, scrags are abhorrent, carnivorous humanoids that prey on humans—or anything else they can sink their teeth into. They're able to regenerate from normal wounds but fear fire most of all. In the wild, they tend to hide in the shallow waters under piers or by the quayside of cities, but some, like Carrackus, find a place in the marginally civilized life of pirates.

TEE-A-NICKNICK

Half human and half qullan, Tee-a-nicknick has never been accepted by either race and has too much of the feral qullan in him to become a peaceful member of human society. He turns to piracy, petty street crime, and ultimately assassination to make a living, and he excels at all three. Tee-a-nicknick is an expert with the blowgun, crafting his own darts from the claws of cats and dipping them in an insidious poison.

BELLANY TUNDASH

Bellany is Sheila Kree's sorceress and brings her talent for offensive magic to *Bloody Keel*'s arsenal. Sheila's most trusted lieutenant, Bellany is the first crewmember to be branded. She was once romantically linked to Morik the Rogue, and she may still have feelings for him—at least, she's gone out of her way to protect him from Sheila Kree.

GAYSELLE WAYFARER

Gayselle is *Bloody Keel*'s deck commander and one of Sheila Kree's most trusted lieutenants—second only after Bellany to be branded with the carved head of Aegis-fang. She favors a short sword and wicked little throwing daggers. When she goes ashore, she takes three of Clan Thump's half-ogres with her, brutes she calls Lumpy, Grumpy, and Dumb-bunny, though their real names are Lorngo, Munjen, and Dembun.

JULE PEPPER

Jule Pepper is one of Sheila Kree's crew but is just as at home as a land-bound highwayman as she is as a seafaring pirate. It's the brand on her shoulder that leads Drizzt and his companions to set out to find Wulfgar and his legendary hammer. Like Bellany, she once had a "close association" with Morik the Rogue, who is obviously drawn to the Sword Coast's most dangerous women.

When asked about her name, she explains, "The jewel sparkles; the pepper spices."

PINOCHET

Captain Pinochet is perhaps the most successful and most feared pirate plying the dangerous waters of the Sword Coast. He maintains a small fleet of ships and associates with any number of wizards and various specialists to aid him in his nefarious endeavors. Pinochet also maintains many key alliances with other underworld figures, including Pasha Pook of Calimport.

A proud and harsh man, he's not above killing his own crewmen to save his skin or even to gain some passing advantage. He's well aware of the reputation of Captain Deudermont's *Sea Sprite*, and their facing off was inevitable. Deudermont ultimately defeats and captures him at the Battle of Asavir's Channel.

ROGUES AND PASHAS OF CALIMPORT

Entreri replaced the dagger in its sheath and leaped up in a rush. "Enjoy the night, little thief. Bask in the cold ocean wind; relish all the sensations of this trip as a man staring death in the face, for Calimport surely spells your doom—and the doom of your friends!" He swept out of the room, banging the door behind him.

—*The Halfling's Gem*

PASHA POOK

Pasha Pook is the remorseless, silver-tongued, and avaricious guildmaster of one of Calimport's most feared thieves' guilds. He came to power largely due to the influence he had over others by use of the enchanted ruby pendant—the same pendant that is eventually stolen from him by Regis. The loss of that magical item is costly to Pook, who sends his finest assassin, Artemis Entreri, after Regis to reclaim it.

But his rise to power wasn't all due to the pendant. Pook is an effective leader who knows when to give a little to get a little more. Though he can be generous, he always makes sure he gets the pick of his guild's take, and when crossed he's an unforgiving and relentless enemy. Always prepared for the inevitable attack on his lofty but tenuous position, Pook keeps a loaded crossbow hidden under his throne—and he knows how to use it.

He leads a life of luxury in his labyrinthine hideout in the neighborhood known as Sholeh Sabban, Sarkh Drudach, in the Khanduq Ward of Calimport, replete with a harem and four hill giant eunuchs as personal bodyguards. The pasha employs wizards, assassins, and even a gang of wererats to patrol the streets for him and to maintain his control over most of the thieves of the sprawling, crowded desert city.

Aside from the ruby pendant, Pook's greatest love is for big cats—he keeps a leopard as a pet—which makes it all the more ironic when he's killed by Guenhwyvar.

LaValle

LaValle is a wizard with a true love of magic. Loyal to Pasha Pook, and perhaps the pasha's most trusted friend, he's most interested in the many ways his association with the guild can help him gain new, more powerful spells.

He works closely with the assassin Artemis Entreri, even employing Entreri for his own purposes. When the rival mage Mancas Tiveros claims authorship of a spell LaValle also claims to have created, LaValle hires Entreri to kill his rival.

LaValle can be more flamboyant than Pook and often chooses spells as much for their dramatic effect as for their utility. He can spy on others through a crystal ball and has wrapped himself in numerous magical defenses, making him a hard man to kill.

Oberon

The wizard Oberon is one of Pasha Pook's lieutenants and also an ally of Artemis Entreri—though his first loyalty is to Pook. He works closely with Entreri and LaValle to help further the schemes and desires of Pasha Pook, occasionally employing a wand that conjures fireballs. The wizard is also a known associate of the pirate captain Pinochet, and he has contacts in the back alleys of half a dozen Sword Coast cities.

SALI DALIB

"What you need, Sali Dalib got," is all anyone needs to know about this shuffling, fast-talking, fidgety merchant. He buys and sells anything and everything, including women, pipeweed, and other illegal—or marginally illegal—goods and services. He's an active fence for stolen property, illicit magic items, forbidden texts, forged documents, and exotic delicacies. The one thing you can always depend on from Sali Dalib is that if you have the coin, he has the merchandise, and he'll try to double-cross you along the way. He's not too good at hiding his duplicity, but thankfully (for his sake) he's got a great talent for getting himself out of trouble.

His assistant is a grim, broken little goblin who's fascinated by magic. Much of his day is spent translating his master's rapid-fire speech to his puzzled customers.

A native of the city, Sali Dalib is convinced that Calimport is the greatest city in the world.

DONDON TIGGERWILLIES

The halfling Dondon Tiggerwillies grew up on the streets of Calimport, stealing to survive. He has become a rather accomplished thief, who uses his halfling stature to disguise himself as a human boy and gain the sympathy, if not trust, of his intended victims. He has experimented with a number of disguises and has found he has quite a talent for it. Now he's known as Calimport's most skilled con artist, even gaining a grudging respect from the locals, who don't interfere as long as he preys only on foreigners.

When Dondon finds himself caught between the assassin Artemis Entreri and the wererat Rassiter, he's seduced by Rassiter's promise of power and allows himself to be infected with lycanthropy. Dondon never really takes to being a wererat the way Rassiter and his gang have and always sees it as a disease—something he suffers through.

Though he once maintained quarters in the Coiled Snake and loved to work the Rogues Circle across from the Spitting Camel, Dondon ends up chained to a wall in a room in his cousin's inn, the Copper Ante.

DWAHVEL TIGGERWILLIES

Dwahvel is a tough, street-smart, and world-wise halfling who runs the Copper Ante. This tavern, gaming house, and festhall in Calimport's Dock Ward is a popular destination for the city's halfling population. What would surprise people most about Dwahvel is that she's a close friend and confidante of Artemis Entreri, acting in some ways as his conscience. She also "cares for" her cousin Dondon—by keeping the wererat chained up in a room in the Copper Ante where he won't be able to cause himself, or her, any further trouble.

THE BASADONI GUILD

SHARLOTTA VESPERS

Standing six feet one inch tall, Sharlotta Vespers is called "Willow Tree" by her guildmaster and lover, Pasha Basadoni. This graceful, striking woman is a gifted assassin and Basadoni's most trusted lieutenant. It's said she was only eight years old when she first killed a man, and that she killed a hundred more in her first two decades of life. Her relationship with the crumbling old guildmaster is only one of the prices she's paid for survival, power, and gold.

KADRAN GORDEON

Another trusted lieutenant of Pasha Basadoni, Kadran Gordeon leads what Basadoni calls his "street militia," a gang of thugs and ruffians who can be called upon to fight for the guild. His men are loyal to him, because he knows how to get to their families.

GIUNTA THE DIVINER

Giunta the Diviner is Basadoni's chief wizard, and as his name would imply, a master of the wizard school of divination. He's able to locate a person merely by touching something the target has recently touched, and he has at his disposal a wide range of divination spells—one of the primary reasons that Basadoni seems to know everything about everybody.

PASHA BASADONI

Leader of a guild to rival Pasha Pook's, Pasha Basadoni has lived a longer life than even he could have predicted, surviving nearly to his nineties. This wizened old assassin was Artemis Entreri's mentor, but unlike Entreri, Basadoni seeks attention and never misses an opportunity to show off his power. Despite his advancing years, he's taken the statuesque assassin Sharlotta Vespers as his lover.

HAND

Hand's real name is unknown—perhaps even to himself—but his street name comes from his uncanny abilities as a pickpocket. He's as quiet and subtle as his art would demand and has been placed in charge of the pickpockets and prostitutes who fall under Basadoni's mastery.

Top to bottom: Sharlotta, Kadran, Giunta, Pasha Basadoni, Hand

DOG PERRY THE HEART

Dog Perry is called "the Heart" because he's known on the streets for being able to slice open his victim's chest so fast that he can remove the mark's still-beating heart and show it to him before he dies. The fact that no one but Dog Perry has ever actually seen this happen has done nothing to quell the rumor, which both Dog Perry and his patron, Quentin Bodeau, use to their full advantage. Though a formidable assassin, Dog Perry is undisciplined and jealous of the more artful Artemis Entreri.

QUENTIN BODEAU

Still convinced that there is honor among thieves, Quentin Bodeau only steals from the rich and only kills when he's forced to. For those two reasons, among others, Quentin broke from Pasha Pook to form his own guild after serving the pasha for two decades. He's a veteran burglar and skilled thief, but he may be a bit too idealistic for the unforgiving streets of the desert city.

RASSITER

Rassiter is the leader of a gang of wererats that dominates the streets of Calimport. He works for Pasha Pook but considers himself the pasha's equal. Obviously, that doesn't sit well with Pook, who is disgusted by this thoroughly off-putting creature. Even Pook's leopard hates Rassiter, who doesn't have much love for the cat either.

The wererat is a survivor, though, who grew up on the streets and kills with a casual disregard for life or honor. Physically bigger than Artemis Entreri and arrogant to a fault, Rassiter often confuses size with power, and that proves his undoing when he ultimately falls to Entreri's blade.

DWARVES OF MITHRAL HALL AND BEYOND

Crenshinibon recognized this wielder, not only a dwarf, but a dwarven priestess, and was not pleased. Dwarves were a stubborn and difficult lot, and resistant to magic. But still, the most evil of artifacts was glad to be out of the snow, glad that someone had returned to Kelvin's Cairn to bear Crenshinibon away.

—Passage to Dawn

THIBBLEDORF PWENT

The wild, almost feral leader of the Gutbuster Brigade, the dwarf battlerager Thibbledorf Pwent is Mithral Hall's single most potent and uncontrollable weapon. Battleragers are trained to charge headlong into a frenzied melee, using their body as a weapon. Pwent's loudly squeaking armor is covered in vicious spikes and blades, and he literally uses every inch of himself as a weapon, grabbing on and tearing his enemies to shreds.

Pwent isn't always a berserk animal, but he always smells like one. Hygiene has never been a priority for dwarves in general, and an intense "personal aroma" is something of a badge of honor for Pwent. Most people find him obnoxious, but anyone who gets to know him and doesn't fall victim to his armor will eventually find a loyal and heartfelt patriot under his steel shell.

The son of Crommower Pwent, who fought alongside Gandalug Battlehammer in the founding days of the clan, Thibbledorf is presumed killed by the dragon Shimmergloom, but he survives to spend nearly two centuries in search of the survivors of Clan Battlehammer.

Though he's always ready to put his head down and barrel into a fight like a wild boar, he's not entirely without brains. Once, when struck by the poisoned dart of a hostile dark elf's hand crossbow, Pwent had the presence of mind to fall to the ground and feign the effects of poison, though a potion protected him. Drawing the drow in closer, he leaped to his feet and did what any good Gutbuster would: ripped the dark elf to bloody shreds.

"Retreat" in any language has never been in Thibbledorf Pwent's vocabulary, and the word will bounce off his battle-hardened skull for the rest of his life.

GANDALUG BATTLEHAMMER

The First King of Mithral Hall, Patron and Founder of Clan Battlehammer, Gandalug's legend kept his descendants going for two thousand years after his presumed death. What none of his survivors knew was that he was not technically dead but was kept in stasis—what he perceived as an endless gray void—by the dark elf matron mother Yvonnel Baenre. Matron Mother Baenre wore one of Gandalug's teeth on a necklace, the dwarf king's spirit entrapped within, for two millennia before inadvertently releasing him in an effort to use his knowledge of Mithral Hall to gain the upper hand on his great-great-great-great grandson, Bruenor.

Upon his glorious return to Mithral Hall, Bruenor insists that Gandalug reclaim his throne, but the First King is reluctant. On Bruenor's insistence, however, Gandalug becomes the Ninth King of Mithral Hall—a post he'll keep only a few years before succumbing to the ravages of age.

GENERAL DAGNA

General Dagna was once the personal attendant of King Harbromm of Citadel Adbar, but he is sent to serve Bruenor in the retaking of Mithral Hall. He stays on as a military advisor but soon becomes a part of Clan Battlehammer, Mithral Hall's military leader, and Bruenor's second in command.

Dagna neither likes nor trusts anyone who isn't a dwarf, and he would go so far, if given the chance, as to drive Drizzt, Catti-brie, Wulfgar, and Regis out of Mithral Hall for good. He winces at the fact that Catti-brie, a human, is allowed to wield Taulmaril and that Wulfgar holds Aegis-fang.

Bruenor is happy to overlook those feelings, though, to benefit from Dagna's centuries of experience on the battlefield.

STUMPET RAKINGCLAW

Stumpet is the only priestess in the service of Mithral Hall, having come from her birthplace, Citadel Adbar, with General Dagna. The service of warlike dwarf gods like Moradin, Dumathoin, and Clangeddin tends to be a male dwarf pursuit, but Stumpet has proven herself first to her gods, then to the male dwarves around her. The dwarves of Clan Battlehammer rally around her when she calls out to her gods. She may not be the most patient priestess, but her capable demeanor gives strength to her king and her clan, and her spells prove potent weapons on the battlefield and equally potent medicine after.

Bruenor honors her by proclaiming her holy water a "nine," and because it is a bit of the ninety-proof, it never freezes.

JERBOLLAH

Vying for a top place in the religious hierarchy of Clan Battlehammer, Jerbollah attempts to brew a holy water that will "properly curl the nose hairs," but he achieves a rating of only seven out of ten from Bruenor. His spells often don't work as precisely as he plans, and an attempt to summon a crimson light has made his face glow red. He's not happy with his progress as a priest.

Actually, Jerbollah's not happy with *anything*.

BUSTER BRACER

Not only is Buster Bracer the most highly regarded armorer of Clan Battlehammer, he is considered one of the finest smiths in all the Realms. He's fashioned armor for Drizzt, Catti-brie, and Regis.

FENDER AND GROLLO

Two valiant dwarves of Clan Battlehammer, Fender and Grollo accompany Catti-brie to Cassius's house in Ten-Towns to retrieve Regis's belongings. Though they both fall victim to the vicious human assassin Artemis Entreri, they fight valiantly to protect their king's adopted daughter. Fender Mallot is considered second only to Bruenor in a fight, but Entreri is still too much for him.

KING HARBROMM

King Harbromm of Citadel Adbar keeps a constant vigil over the Spine of the World, always preparing the dwarves of his clan for battle against the orc hordes and other enemies that lurk in the mountains above and the Underdark below. And that's not just paranoia—Citadel Adbar has been besieged by orc hordes, some as large as a hundred thousand strong, more than a hundred times.

He has sworn allegiance to Bruenor, even sending his most trusted advisor, Dagna, to Mithral Hall to serve Clan Battlehammer. He's also closely allied with Silverymoon and is a trusted friend of Alustriel, though everyone knows his first loyalty is to his dwarves.
King Harbromm's steadfast honor is a shining example for all the people of the North.

IVAN AND PIKEL BOULDERSHOULDER

The Bouldershoulder brothers, Ivan and Pikel, are friends of the priest Cadderly and join him on his many adventures far to the south around the Spirit Soaring. Though Ivan is what many would consider a "typical" dwarf, his eccentric—most would say completely insane—brother Pikel is far from it. Pikel is a druid—or, as he pronounces it, "doo dad"—and though at first the assumption is that he just *thinks* he's a druid, when he casts spells, they actually work!

CITADEL ADBAR

Citadel Adbar, named for its first king, is a dwarven hold east of Longsaddle and Silverymoon that was old even in the first era of Mithral Hall. Led by the indomitable King Harbromm, the dwarves of Citadel Adbar are as hardworking, fun loving, and battle ready as any dwarf could be. Eight thousand of them, the fierce Iron Guard, march to battle in support of Bruenor's efforts to reclaim Mithral Hall, and many stay on to help repopulate Clan Battlehammer.

Citadel Adbar is home to some twenty thousand dwarves, and its tower, which roils with smoke and forge-fire, can be seen from miles around, but most of the citadel is underground—a maze of forges, workshops, and smithies.

THE CREW OF *BOTTOM FEEDER*

Bottom Feeder is a twenty-foot, square-bottomed riverboat that is atypical in many ways, most of all in that it was built and is crewed by dwarves. She plies the waters of the River Chionthar from the city of Baldur's Gate east to Scornubel and as far as Iriaebor. They often have to fight off attacks by goblins, bandits, and other threats, so the four-dwarf crew has trained in the use of crossbows, which they keep handy in a locker on the boat's deck.

Standing: *Bumpo* and *Donat*, seated: *Yipper* and *Quipper*

CAPTAIN BUMPO THUNDERPUNCHER

Bumpo is *Bottom Feeder*'s captain and a fierce admirer of Bruenor, though the dwarf king is surprised to hear that his reputation has spread as far south as Baldur's Gate. It may be true that dwarves hate water, but then not all dwarves are exactly the same, and Bumpo and his brother and cousins prove that every day.

DONAT THUNDERPUNCHER

Donat Thunderpuncher is more at home on the water than any of his kind, including his brother and cousins. He's a fairly accomplished navigator and never shies from a fight. Donat knows all the ins and outs of the river, including all the places goblins like to hide.

YIPPER AND QUIPPER FISHQUISHER

The brothers Yipper and Quipper Fishquisher are Bumpo and Donat's cousins. They crew *Bottom Feeder*, pushing along the bottom and banks of the River Chionthar with long poles. Like Bumpo and Donat, they're always ready to drop their poles and pick up crossbows to defend their boat.

PEOPLE OF ICEWIND DALE AND THE NORTH

LUSKAN

Also known as the City of Sails, Luskan is located at the mouth of the Mirar River, just south of the western tip of the Spine of the World Mountains on the coast of the Sea of Swords. Home to some fifteen thousand people, it's smaller than some of the other Sword Coast cities, especially Waterdeep. The city is surrounded by a strong curtain wall and guarded by spear- and crossbow-armed guards, who are reluctant to open the gates for just anyone. Merchants are generally allowed in to trade in the city's open-air markets or to ship their goods from the bustling, if dangerous, docks.

The dockside isn't safe, especially at night, when rogues, pirates, and inhuman creatures prey on the small, weak, or drunk, hiding in the fog that perpetually rolls in from the sea. Laws are inconsistently enforced in Luskan, but when thieves are captured, their punishments can be particularly cruel, including public torture and execution at the so-called Prisoners' Carnival.

The true power in Luskan is held by the Arcane Brotherhood, a cabal of powerful wizards based in the Hosttower of the Arcane, a structure that dominates the city's skyline.

MORIK THE ROGUE

Morik the Rogue is a well-known thief and information broker who knows everyone in Luskan, though not everyone in Luskan knows him. A master of disguise, Morik operates under many aliases that he uses to infiltrate different parts of society. He's a pragmatic man who makes decisions carefully, but he still can be led by his heart. He doesn't make friends easily, but when he does, he can be surprisingly loyal for a man raised on the mean streets of this rough-and-tumble port city. Friends aside, the true love of Morik's life may be the city of Luskan itself.

ARUMN GARDPECK

Arumn Gardpeck is the owner of one of Luskan's most popular seaside dives, the Cutlass, on Half-Moon Street. He's a practical sort, who's accustomed to dealing with sailors, pirates, and lowlife dock rats, but all that seediness never crept into his psyche. A kind if stern man, he feels as strongly for the well-being of his staff—especially Delly, who's like a daughter to him—as for the tavern itself.

DELLY CURTIE

Delenia Curtie's friends call her "Delly," though she hasn't got too many friends. Delly works as a barmaid at the Cutlass, where she serves drinks to pirates, thieves, and dockworkers. Young and still immature, she has a good heart and a certain innocent quality that causes some men to want to take care of her. No matter how rough things get at the Cutlass, no one bothers Delly—Arumn Gardpeck and the tavern's regulars make sure of it.

Delly's favorite time of day, a time she reserves for herself, is dusk, which she calls her "quiet hour."

JOSI PUDDLES

Josi Puddles is a regular at the Cutlass and a friend of Arumn Gardpeck. He's something of a hanger-on, never really making his mark on the world. Though his jealousy of Wulfgar grows and grows as the barbarian is taken deeper into Arumn's confidence, no one would have guessed that Josi would ever work up the nerve to steal the mighty warhammer Aegis-fang and sell it to the pirate captain Sheila Kree.

Lucky to have survived that mistake, Josi can still be found at the Cutlass and doesn't seem to be going anywhere. He has always harbored a secret love for Delly Curtie, a love that will forever go unrequited.

Whisper

Whisper can be found at the end of an alley guarded by crossbowmen. From her safehouse there, she deals in information, one of Luskan's most valuable commodities. With her reputation as a survivor of the roughest neighborhoods—a street-smart fixer who deals every day with murderers, thugs, and cutpurses—it can be a surprise to find that she's a young, attractive woman. She hardly comes across as the coin-hungry mercenary she is. One of the ways she uses her feminine wiles is to help her choose her fights wisely and well.

Sydney

Lusting after power, determined to raise her personal status, desirous of the favor and attention of her mentor, Sydney is a young wizard on the rise at Luskan's Hosttower of the Arcane. Though only in her mid-twenties, she's earned an apprenticeship with Dendybar, one of the most accomplished of the Hosttower's mages. When she is assigned by Dendybar to keep an eye on Artemis Entreri, Sydney identifies the assassin as a powerful ally. She does the same with Harkle Harpell, and though she's basically incapable of sincere emotion, she manages to string the older wizard along with a thin facade of romantic interest.

Not that Sydney has much in the way of feminine wiles. She hasn't much interest in her physical appearance, being more interested in power, wealth, and station.

Dendybar the Mottled

Master of the North Spire of the Hosttower of the Arcane, Dendybar the Mottled is one of the five most powerful wizards of the Arcane Brotherhood. He's a highly intelligent and experienced man, with enormous magical resources at his beck and call, but all that power has separated him from what it means to be human, and he's come to value knowledge over life.

It is his ambition and outspoken desire to rise to the position of archmage that leads him to manipulate the young apprentice Akar Kessell into murdering Dendybar's chief rival, the former Master of the North Spire, Morkai the Red. And though Morkai frightens Dendybar even in death, Dendybar summons Morkai's spirit to provide him with information—even knowing that, one day, Morkai will slip the bounds of his magical compulsion and attack him.

Though he appears to be a frail old man, in truth his power is considerable. And his lust for still more knows no bounds.

ELDELUC

A young wizard from Luskan's Hosttower of the Arcane, Eldeluc has allied himself with Dendybar and helps his master convince Akar Kessell to kill Morkai. Where Dendybar appears frail but is master of extraordinary magic, Eldeluc is physically strong and intimidating, but his magic is no match for Dendybar's.

MORKAI THE RED

Morkai the Red is the Master of the North Tower of the Hosttower of the Arcane in Luskan, and an associate of Alustriel, until he is murdered in the far-off town of Easthaven by his own apprentice, Akar Kessell—a man he treated as his own son for a quarter of a century. But it is Dendybar the Mottled who puts Akar up to it, and when Morkai crosses over, Dendybar keeps his spirit bound as a specter.

Though the undead Morkai is compelled to serve his hateful master, he takes great pleasure in confounding Dendybar at every turn, couching his answers in riddles and half-truths. He remains Dendybar's most valuable informant nonetheless. Being summoned into a conjuring chamber he created himself doesn't make his service to Dendybar go down any easier, and Morkai constantly plans for the day the spell will break.

JIERDAN

Jierdan is a guardsman assigned to Luskan's north gate, but he also works for Dendybar. It is Jierdan who convinces the Nightkeeper to allow the dark elf Drizzt and his companions into the city—only so he can follow them on Dendybar's orders in hopes of recovering the Crystal Shard for his greedy master. When he's forced to work and travel with Artemis Entreri, a rivalry develops on their way to Silverymoon. Though Sydney calls Jierdan "honorable," very few others would agree.

Barbarians of Icewind Dale

King Heafstaag

Son of Hrothulf the Strong and grandson of Angaar the Brave, Heafstaag is the hereditary king of the Tribe of the Elk. Known as a fierce warrior, he bears the scars of a life spent on the windswept plains of Icewind Dale. He lost an eye to a reindeer's antler, and his left hand was crippled by a raging polar bear. Like most of his kin, he loathes wizards, and though he is compelled to ally himself with Akar Kessell, he never likes the mage. His mother was a "civilized" woman from Luskan, who was taken captive as a child in a caravan raid and raised by the Tribe of the Elk. She died never having returned to the city of her birth. Heafstaag is eventually killed by Wulfgar in single combat, after Wulfgar invokes the Right of Challenge.

Revjak

Revjak, son of Jorn the Red, is the first barbarian of the Tribe of the Elk to greet Wulfgar when the Son of Beornegar comes to challenge Heafstaag. He had been friends with Wulfgar's father, and after the death of Heafstaag, Revjak, who always remains in control of his emotions, brings a sense of calm to the ensuing chaos. Revjak eventually unifies the nomadic barbarian tribes and strengthens their ties with the people of Ten-Towns. Though he'll never admit it to his tribe, Revjak holds a secret fondness for "the civilized life" and longs to visit the cities of the Sword Coast.

JEREK WOLF SLAYER

Jerek Wolf Slayer is the chief of the Sky Ponies, a tribe of
barbarians who revere the god Uthgar and their totem animal,
the pegasus. Jerek is as proud and as regal as the rest of his people,
but he's also as xenophobic and as unwelcoming of outsiders.

TORLIN

Torlin, son of Jerek, is being groomed to one day hold his father's
place as leader of the Sky Ponies. Valric often holds him up as an
example of the strong future of their tribe and has even granted
him the high honor of being imbued with the spirit of the pegasus
in their wild tribal rituals. Only Wulfgar has ever beaten Torlin in a
test of strength.

VALRIC HIGH EYE

No one's sure precisely how old Valric High Eye actually is, but
he is ancient indeed. Still, he shows no signs of slowing down
and serves the Sky Ponies as their shaman with the vigor and
enthusiasm of a boy. He is a wise if impetuous spiritual advisor,
leading the tribe in their worship of Uthgar. He has the ability
to summon the pegasus, the Sky Ponies' totem animal.

Top to bottom: *Jerek, Torlin, Valric*

KIERSTAAD

Born in the Year of the Bright Blade (1347 DR), Kierstaad, son of Revjak, is only seventeen years old when he first
encounters Wulfgar. He comes to idolize Wulfgar and provides a great hope that the barbarians of Icewind Dale will
continue to embrace civilized ways in the next generation.

BEORNEGAR

Beornegar, son of Beorne, is Wulfgar's father. He has spent much of his life collecting tales of the great treasure horde
of the white dragon, Dracos Icingdeath, and he passes those stories on to his son. Beornegar even finds a secret
entrance into the wyrm's lair, but dies in battle before he is able to face off against mighty Icingdeath. That is a task that
eventually falls to his valiant son.

Left to right: *Kierstaad, Beornegar, Berkthgar*

BERKTHGAR THE BOLD

Berkthgar, son of Beothgin, is the chieftain of the barbarian village
of Settlestone. Unnerved by magic, stubborn, and short-tempered,
Berkthgar follows the old ways, even continuing to think of the
dwarves of Mithral Hall and the villagers of Ten-Towns as his
enemies. He's so old fashioned that he's easily stymied by strong
women, whom he does not approve of as warriors. But one special
woman, Catti-brie, has managed to chip away some of that rough
facade. Berkthgar shares the nobility and passion of his people and
loves nothing more than to lead his hordes into battle, singing the
praises of his god, Tempus, Lord of Battles, all the way.

The Harpells

The Harpells are a clan of eccentric wizards that lives in the Ivy Mansion—a compound of buildings near an uphill-flowing stream outside the village of Longsaddle. Having lived there for more years than anyone can count, their collective knowledge of the history and geography of the North is second to none. Though the Harpells are known throughout the Silver Marches for their good-natured eccentricity and hospitality, most beings prefer to give the Ivy Mansion a wide berth. At least one of their clan, Matherly Harpell, fell victim to his own experiments, when a certain mixture of potions left him petrified—forever a statue in the Ivy Mansion. The uphill-flowing steam was the work of Chardin Harpell, now a very, very old man, who spends his time wandering the grounds mumbling to himself.

Harkle Harpell

The current patriarch, such as he is, of the Harpell family, Harkle is a wise and venerable wizard with a few little quirks that can also make him extremely dangerous to be around. Though Drizzt has learned to trust his advice, he's also learned to be ready for anything where Harkle is concerned. The wizard's spells tend to fail, often with disastrous results—showers of sparks, flashing bolts of searing lightning, and fire . . . lots of fire—and he usually ends up hurting himself. Still, when they work, Harkle's spells can be extremely potent, and he's capable of deadly offensive magic.

Harkle tends to ramble when he speaks, and it's easy to get frustrated with his meandering thought processes, but he's at heart an honorable man, unable or unwilling to keep secrets or tell lies. A welcoming and generous host, he's always willing to help when help is needed.

Bella don DelRoy Harpell

Bella don DelRoy Harpell is the daughter of DelRoy Harpell, who is the eldest of the clan and the leader of the village of Longsaddle. She's a curious and capable mage, and though barely more than five feet tall, her lightning bolts pack a serious punch. None too fond of illithids, Bella is even less fond of people who mistake her for a halfling.

BIDDERDOO HARPELL

Harkle's cousin Bidderdoo spent seven years as the Harpell family pet after a bad mix of potions turned him into a dog. During the Time of Troubles, he gathered the necessary components to change himself back, though most of his family liked him better as a dog. The transformation is still ongoing, and Bidderdoo is known to bury things, and often reacts to danger with a bark. Too many enemies are fooled by that kind of eccentric behavior into thinking that Bidderdoo is mad, or a fool, but not only is he actually a werewolf, he's a powerful spellcaster on top of it. If he can't kill you with a spell, he'll rip your throat out with his teeth.

REGWELD HARPELL

Regweld Harpell is obsessed with breeding different animals with horses to create better mounts. The occasional exploding alchemy shop and feral creature of nightmare later, he ends up with the half-horse, half-frog he calls Puddlejumper. Astride this bizarre mount, Regweld leads the forces of Longsaddle in the battle of Keeper's Dale. And though he fights bravely, never having such excitement in his life, he is brought down by a trio of lightning bolts and is mourned as a hero.

MALCHOR HARPELL

Another of Harkle's cousins, Malchor Harpell doesn't share his family's eccentric ways, and neither does he share their home. Malchor resides in the mysterious Tower of Twilight, a keep that exists in a dimension all its own that comes into view only at twilight. Its door remains behind on the Prime Material Plane but can only be found by those who are showed the way by Malchor. The tower is a needlelike spire that tapers to a point at the top and is reached by a bridge of green light.

Malchor has advised many kings, and though he comes across as arrogant and brusque, he has a fine sense of humor and a steady, disciplined way of looking at things. He gave the scimitar Twinkle to Drizzt Do'Urden and is a close associate of Khelben "Blackstaff" Arunsun, so he's known to work for the cause of good, but only on his own terms. His apprentice is the teenaged son of a wealthy landowner who has forsaken his own name and taken a vow of silence that Malchor believes will teach him discipline.

UNDERBRIDGE/OVERBRIDGE

A sprawling compound on the outskirts of Longsaddle, the Ivy Mansion is the ancestral estate of the Harpell family. A stream flows uphill from the town below, and the bridge that crosses it is no less bizarre. The bridge arches high above the water, unadorned even by handrails. To gain access to the mansion, you have to walk along the underside of the bridge, which seems to possess its own answer to gravity, then walk along the top to leave. Why? Even the Harpells don't know for sure.

Villagers of Ten-Towns

Cassius of Bryn Shander

The spokesman from the largest of Ten-Towns, Bryn Shander, Cassius is one of the most powerful men in Icewind Dale. He supports forming an army to defend against Akar Kessell and is so impressed with Regis that he gives the halfling his huge house in Bryn Shander—then immediately regrets it, suspecting that Regis might have used his ruby pendant to arrange the gift. When Regis goes off to join Bruenor in the quest for Mithral Hall, Cassius reclaims his home.

Cassius appears to always be scanning his surroundings, his eyes moving as quickly as his active mind. He was a rogue, having grown up as a street urchin in Luskan, before settling in Bryn Shander, and his thief's ways are still just below the surface. Still, he's a trusted and capable leader and has been named elderman, the voice of all of Ten-Towns.

Jensin Brent of Caer-Dineval

Spokesman of the town of Caer-Dineval, young Jensin is a capable fighter, and he distinguishes himself in the Battle of Icewind Dale. He's smart and even-tempered and takes his position very seriously, but Schermont, who tries from time to time to goad him into escalating the tensions between their rival fisheries, can intimidate him.

Kemp of Targos

Kemp is the spokesman for Targos, the second largest, and with Bryn Shander, the only other walled community of Ten-Towns. As such he's the second most powerful member of the council and often opposes Cassius. He is distrustful of outsiders, especially non-humans, though he's enough of a merchant to set those feelings aside and work with Clan Battlehammer to broker their ore. Kemp is extremely reluctant to see Targos or the rest of Ten-Towns dragged into conflict with the barbarians or with any of the other forces around them. War, like racism, is bad for trade.

Muldoon of Lonelywood

Muldoon took on the role of spokesman for the town of Lonelywood when Regis stepped down. Born in Waterdeep, he came to Lonelywood as a child when his father "was asked to leave the city," and in time Muldoon became a skilled negotiator and successful merchant. A few years later, his father left for Waterdeep with a caravan and never returned.

Schermont of Caer-Konig

Stern and heavy-handed, Schermont is perhaps the least personable of the spokesmen of Ten-Towns, and like a majority of the villagers he represents, he still holds a grudge against their rivals in Caer-Dineval. Schermont succeeded Dorim Lugar as spokesman of the town of Caer-Konig when the latter was killed in a battle with a rival fishing boat from Caer-Dineval on the waters of Lac Dinneshere.

Agorwal of Termalaine

The owner of a mine that produces the gems that gave his town its name, Agorwal is proud to have been the first to make a kill in the battle of Bryn Shander, but that pride is short lived. The spokesman from Termalaine is soon killed by Akar Kessell's forces. Drizzt considered Agorwal a friend.

Glensather of Easthaven

As spokesman for the town of Easthaven, Glensather is a capable and even-tempered leader, well respected by all who know him. He dies in the Battle of Icewind Dale, defending the towns he loved: a cluster of little villages that he sees as sturdy bulwarks against barbarism, and the best hope for bringing civilization to Icewind Dale.

THE FIEFDOM OF AUCKNEY

Like Auckney itself, a village of two hundred people that rarely showed up on any maps, the castle was of modest design. There were a dozen rooms for the family, and for Temigast, of course, and another five for the half-dozen servants and ten soldiers who served at the place. A pair of low and squat towers anchored the castle, barely topping fifteen feet, for the wind always blew strongly in Auckney. A common joke was, if the wind ever stopped blowing, all the villagers would fall over forward, so used were they to leaning as they walked.

—The Spine of the World

LORD FERINGAL AUCK

The kindly young lord of Auckney is a quiet and gentle man who has been lord since the age of fourteen, after the deaths of his parents. He's not a terribly effective leader, but Auckney's such a small and out-of-the-way place, he doesn't really need to be. For important matters of state he depends on the advice of Steward Temigast, and his sister Priscilla keeps him abreast of social niceties. But still, he's a lonely and romantic young man, smitten by the beautiful peasant girl Meralda Ganderlay.

LADY PRISCILLA AUCK

Lord Feringal's older sister Priscilla is the only one who calls him Feri, and if you ask Feringal, that's one person too many. She is shrewish and manipulative, outwardly looking to protect her brother from a scandalous marriage to a peasant girl, but in fact she's just trying to control Feringal and the fiefdom she feels she should have been allowed to rule.

MERALDA

Meralda is the daughter of Dohni and Biaste Ganderlay, simple farmers from the remote fiefdom of Auckney. Naturally pretty, Meralda has drawn the attention of two very different men: the roguish peasant Jaka Sculi and Lord Feringal Auck, the richest and most powerful man in the fiefdom. She loves Jaka, but Feringal will save her family from another generation of poverty. When she becomes pregnant with Jaka's baby, she blames Wulfgar, accusing him of rape—an accusation she will someday recant, but not until after the barbarian adopts her illegitimate baby, the girl named Colson, as his own.

STEWARD TEMIGAST

Temigast came to Auckney from Waterdeep in the Year of the Weeping Moon (1339 DR) first as a merchant then as a trusted counselor for Lord Feringal's father, Lord Tristan Auck. He helped raise Feringal and Priscilla when their parents died, advising them in such a way that, though they bicker with each other over social matters, the fiefdom is well looked after and peaceful. A worldly gentleman, Temigast can often be found on the rocky coasts near Auckney, painting seascapes.

JAKA SCULI

Jaka Sculi came to Auckney from Luskan in the Year of the Sword (1365 DR) with his mother, who is a distant descendant of the mercenary princes of the now-forgotten Blade Kingdoms. She was born with a silver spoon in her mouth but was unable to do the same for Jaka, who grew up feeling he was better than the people around him, though he did nothing to actually earn the respect he demanded. He courts Meralda only after learning that Feringal wants her too. When he slips off the edge of a cliff, making a dramatic if insincere appeal to Meralda, his frivolous life is brought to an end.

LIAM WOODGATE

Liam Woodgate is Lord Feringal's carriage driver and bodyguard, though he may not look the part. Though barely larger than a human toddler, Liam is no child. He's a tough ex-soldier and a staunch defender of his lord and master. The gnomes who settled in Auckney were not welcomed at first, so they had to work extra hard for acceptance. Liam is a perfect example of the sort of hard-won respect and work ethic that defines the gnomes of Auckney.

SILVERYMOON AND THE CHOSEN

KHELBEN "BLACKSTAFF" ARUNSUN

Khelben can be encountered in Silverymoon but is actually one of the secret lords of Waterdeep, where he serves as the city's Blackstaff, or archmage. Though he presents himself as a simple adventurer, always casual in demeanor, he's a Chosen of Mystra and perhaps the most powerful spellcaster in all the Realms, on par with the likes of Elminster or Telemont Tanthul. The signature black staff that he carries exhibits an array of different powers. It's believed that there is actually more than one such artifact and that Khelben chooses a new one every time he leaves his home, Blackstaff Tower, in the heart of Waterdeep.

DOVE FALCONHAND

One of Alustriel's sisters and also a Chosen of Mystra, Dove Falconhand does not live full-time in Silverymoon but visits often. She is a powerful spellcaster in her own right and, as one of the fabled Seven Sisters, also possesses Mystra's silver fire. Dove is a ranger and is skilled with a bow. She's as stubborn and headstrong as she is agile, and she hates the formality of Silverymoon's court.

FREDEGAR "FRET" ROCKCRUSHER

The exception that proves the rule, Fredegar Rockcrusher is perhaps the least typical dwarf in all the Realms. Obsessed with cleanliness and found buried in books rather than toiling at a forge, Fredegar is a scholar of some renown and the self-proclaimed "best-loved sage" of Lady Alustriel of Silverymoon.

His most influential work has been done in the field of inter-species relations, making him the foremost expert on demihumans and humanoids in the North, if not in all of Faerûn. Though he was born in Citadel Adbar, he's spent many years in Silverymoon effecting more human manners. There he's come to trust in Lady Alustriel's magic, and he is a trusted advisor for both Alustriel and her sister, Dove Falconhand.

ALUSTRIEL

The Lady of Silverymoon, Alustriel is one of the Seven Sisters. She is a wizard of extraordinary power, Chosen of Mystra, the goddess of magic. Like the other Chosen, Alustriel is effectively immortal and possesses Mystra's silver fire—an innate magical ability of enormous destructive power. She wields that power, as she does all things, with great care and diligence. A staunch defender of Silverymoon, she will choose her city's safety above other considerations, but she is still a steadfast ally of Bruenor, and she and Drizzt share a bond that may be a little more than respectful—maybe even a little more than friendly.

SILVERYMOON

Silverymoon is a shining beacon of all that's best in the Realms. Its wide and winding tree-lined thoroughfares are peopled with humans, elves, dwarves, halflings, and representatives of dozens of other races, all living in peace and harmony. The architecture is a mix of human and elven, with graceful towers and soaring spires gleaming in the sun. The Vault of Sages is one of the Realms' most highly regarded libraries, and scholars from across Faerûn come there to study.

THE CHOSEN OF MYSTRA

A special handful of the most powerful spellcasters in the Realms draws the attention of the goddess of magic and is granted extraordinary powers—and extraordinary responsibility. The Chosen of Mystra are wizards who have merged with the Weave—the unifying force created by Mystra that binds magic to her will—and have become immortal beings in her service. They possess her silver fire, a magic power with almost limitless offensive capability, and most are marked by the silver hair of their goddess's avatar.

TERRIEN DOUCARD

Terrien succeeds Besnell as the leader of Silverymoon's Knights in Silver. He has dedicated his life to preserving Silverymoon. Though he's in love with Alustriel, Terrien knows better than to act on those feelings. His father, an elf, was a cousin of Besnell, and his mother was the second daughter of one of Silverymoon's wealthiest families.

BESNELL

Besnell is a high-ranking elf in Silverymoon's Knights in Silver. A proud man, he truly loves Silverymoon and is known for his high spirits and sincere desire for peace. He utters his last words: "For the good of all goodly folk," at the end of the Battle of Icewind Dale.

SEA SPRITE

Drizzt Do'Urden stood on the very edge of the beam, as far forward as he could go, one hand grasping tight the guide rope of the flying jib. This ship was a smooth runner, perfect in balance and ballast and with the best of crews, but the sea was rough this day and Sea Sprite cut and bounced through the rolls at full sail, throwing a heavy spray.

—Passage to Dawn

CAPTAIN DEUDERMONT

Nothing strikes fear into the heart of a Sword Coast pirate more than the name Deudermont. With his highly trained and fiercely loyal crew, Deudermont's *Sea Sprite* was purpose-built as a pirate hunter. Her captain is a very successful merchant with a palatial home in Waterdeep to prove it, but he has been hunting pirates for years now, with exceptional results.

Sea Sprite's captain is a fair but practical man with a strong sense of justice. His deep respect for the sea is matched only by his total dedication to his crew. Deudermont judges people by their character alone, going so far as to embrace a certain dark elf. He and Drizzt have been close friends ever since—a friendship based on a shared respect for justice.

Though he's well known and highly respected by the finer folk of the Sword Coast cities—even in Luskan, where he's welcomed as a hero in the homes of the aristocracy—he's made more than his share of enemies. Pirates and thieves across the Sword Coast would love nothing more than to see him dead, and there's a standing bounty of ten thousand gold pieces on his head in the darker alleyways of Luskan.

ROBILLARD

Robillard is *Sea Sprite's* wizard, Captain Deudermont's most trusted associate, and is widely considered to be the finest ship's mage on the Sword Coast. He can use his spells to fill *Sea Sprite's* sails with wind or to deflate a pirate's sails. He's been known to employ destructive lightning bolts and fireballs, and he can imbue others with the ability to fly. Robillard is suspicious of just about everyone, fully aware of the plans of his captain's many enemies. He doesn't like it when Deudermont goes ashore in Luskan and can be protective of him even at sea.

WAILLAN MICANTY

Waillan Micanty, the youngest member of *Sea Sprite*'s crew, is typical of the fiercely loyal pirate hunters whom Captain Deudermont employs. He shares Robillard's protective streak and has a dead-eye aim on the ship's ballista.

GRIMSLEY

Grimsley is *Sea Sprite*'s rudder crew chief and a perfect example of the fine seamanship found aboard Captain Deudermont's ship. Born in the Year of the Fist (1311 DR), he's been at sea since he turned ten, and he has served with Deudermont since the Year of Moonfall (1344 DR). He stopped counting when Deudermont or another of his crewmates saved his life for the hundredth time, and he promptly vowed never to serve another captain.

SEA SPRITE

Captain Deudermont's pirate-chasing schooner was built by the finest naval architects and sea wizards of Waterdeep. Funded by the secret lords of Waterdeep, *Sea Sprite* and her captain were charged with patrolling the vital Sword Coast shipping lanes from Calimport in the south to Luskan in the north. She flies the banner of Waterdeep when she sails north of Baldur's Gate and flies Calimport's flag south of Baldur's Gate. The three-masted schooner is light and sleek in the water and one of the fastest ships on any sea. A flying deck in the stern sports a large ballista mounted on a pivot, and smaller heavy crossbows are mounted forward. Her crew of forty lives and dies by Deudermont's command. When the order "Killer banner up!" is cried from the crow's nest, it means a pirate vessel has been sighted, and the chase is on.

THE NORTH AND BEYOND

MONTOLIO DEBROUCHEE

Montolio deBrouchee, known as "Mooshie" to his friends, is the blind ranger who trains Drizzt and is the dark elf's first friend on the World Above. He has spent his life as a servant of the nature goddess Mielikki, having been trained by the ranger Dilamon. As a member of the Rangewalkers, Montolio fought in numerous wars—enough to know that he prefers peace—spent a winter trapped on a mountainside, and finally lost his eyesight to the searing breath of a red dragon.

Blind, and crippled with self-pity, he went out into the wilderness on his own, settling in what would soon be known as Mooshie's Grove, just waiting to die. But there he discovers the evil plans of the orc chief Graul and rededicates himself to combating Graul and his orc hordes. In the ensuing years he develops a burning hatred for orcs.

Montolio is a good man and a skilled ranger despite his blindness. His other senses heightened to compensate for his blindness, and he enlists the aid of two animal familiars, the owl Hooter and the brown bear Bluster.

Montolio teaches Drizzt not only the ways of the ranger and the beliefs of Mielikki but also teaches him values like trust and loyalty and skills such as how to speak the Common Tongue of the World Above. When Montolio finally dies of old age, Drizzt leaves Mooshie's Grove but will never forget a single one of the lessons of his first human friend.

CADDERLY BONADUCE

Though he is only twenty-nine years of age, Cadderly appears much older. He sacrificed some of his life-force to build the glorious Spirit Soaring, a temple devoted to Denier, the god he serves as a priest. He is a cleric with power and wisdom well beyond his years, and Drizzt is convinced that he has the ability to destroy Crenshinibon.

LADY DANICA BONADUCE

Lady Danica is Cadderly's wife and mother of their twin sons. She was trained in the ways of the monk by Grandmaster Penpahg d'Ahn and is as skilled and disciplined a warrior as Cadderly is a priest. They live together in the Spirit Soaring.

KELLINDIL

Kellindil is an elf archer who lives with his family in the mountains not far from Dead Orc Pass. He hates drow but hates even more doing harm to creatures that don't deserve it. He captures Roddy McGristle, but McGristle is freed by Tephanis. The quickling distracts the elf just long enough for McGristle to grab Kellindil from behind and strangle him.

TARATHIEL

Tarathiel is a moon elf who lives in the Moonwood. He is a skilled archer and a staunch defender of his people. The sight of a lone drow wandering the North is more than enough to pique his interest, and he's been following Drizzt for some time.

E'KRESSA THE SEER

E'kressa is a diviner who hires out his services to anyone with the proper coin. His divination spells are effective, and as such he's amassed a fair fortune. The gnome lives in an imposing house that is protected by an array of spells and a small army of gargoyles. Though his eyesight is fine, he pretends to be blind "to impress the peasants."

THE GREAT WYRMS

Even if they had to rely only on their physical strength, the dragons of Faerûn would be among the most dangerous creatures known, but they are more than just monstrous lizards. The great wyrms are intelligent beings, often empowered with impressive magic. These ancient creatures live for thousands of years and continue to grow throughout their life spans. Most, especially the evil chromatic dragons, are greedy hoarders of magnificent treasures, while the metallics are goodly beings that work to better human life. Either way, dragons tend to keep their own counsel, remaining mysterious and aloof from a world that regards them with fear and respect.

HEPHAESTUS

Named for an obscure god of blacksmiths, Hephaestus is a proud but lazy red dragon that has inhabited a network of caves near the city of Mirabar for centuries. Unlike most red dragons, Hephaestus is easy to fool, not terribly smart, and willing to work with humans. He provides smelting services—with the aid of his fiery breath—for exorbitant fees. Still, he's been known to devour the occasional merchant or passerby, and says he's particularly fond of the taste of paladins. He is known alternately as the Destroyer of Cockelby, The Devourer of Ten Thousand Cattle, and He Who Crushed Angelander the Stupid Silver.

RED DRAGONS

Evil wyrms that revel in chaos and destruction, red dragons are the largest of their kind. They are known for their greed—amassing enormous treasure hordes—and for their temperamental and arrogant nature. Their subterranean lairs are hot and stink of sulfur, the smell of their fiery breath that can burn virtually anything it touches to cinders. Red dragons are generally found in temperate and sub-tropical mountains.

WHITE DRAGONS

Arctic wyrms breathe streams of frigid air that can instantly freeze a living creature. Brutish and feral, the white dragons are the least intelligent of the chromatic dragons. They're also among the greediest and are able to live off the love of their hordes for decades at a time. When they do eat, they insist on food that has been frozen. Frost giants are a particular delicacy. White dragon lairs are found in arctic and sub-arctic environments, deep in ice caves.

ICINGDEATH

The barbarians of Icewind Dale considered the white dragon Icingdeath to be but a legend, a tall tale to scare children. But the great white wyrm is no legend. Dracos Icingdeath is the common name for the dragon Ingeloakastimizilian, who crawled into his freezing lair one day and went to sleep for so long that when he awoke, he had grown too big to crawl back out through the narrow tunnels. Content to stay in his lair, surrounded by his massive treasure horde and covered in a layer of ice, Icingdeath spends decades without even moving.

But that lonely slumber is interrupted by Wulfgar, who finds Icingdeath's lair and challenges the dragon. With the help of Drizzt, Wulfgar kills Icingdeath and takes his horde for the aid of the people of Icewind Dale. Drizzt claims a scimitar from the dragon's horde that still bears the wyrm's name.

SHADOW DRAGONS

The breath of a shadow dragon drains the life-essence from its victims. The wyrms are creatures that exist in part in the Plane of Shadow and in part in the deepest reaches of the Underdark. A shadow dragon, despite their enormous size, can be difficult to spot from a distance. Their jet black scales shimmer with color, and they're surrounded by shadows. A shadow dragon can disappear into the Shadow Fringe at will and can command masses of shadow creatures to serve its will. Most of them are also spellcasters, preferring illusions to attract their prey.

SHIMMERGLOOM

When the shadow dragon Shimmergloom moves up from the Underdark into the lower caverns beneath Mithral Hall, he routs an entire dwarf army and feasts on his victims. He then sleeps for centuries, served by slaves who know better than to wake their wicked master. Though he's finally defeated by Bruenor and his companions when Mithral Hall is retaken, Shimmergloom was the hall's master for longer than any proud dwarf would like to admit.

SILVER DRAGONS

These goodly dragons are able to take human shape at will and seem to prefer that form. They often maintain close personal relationships with humans, occasionally even accepting leadership roles within a human community. They don't always reveal the fact that they're actually dragons, but though that may seem dishonest, their motives are invariably beneficial. The metallic plates on their heads lend them the nickname "shield dragons."

MERGANDEVINASANDER OF CHULT

A mighty black dragon with hypnotic purple eyes, Mergandevinasander lives deep in the primeval jungles of faraway Chult. He was hatched in the Year of the Hunting Ghosts (659 DR) far to the south in Zakhara. Ejected from his mother's lair as a wyrmling, he wandered the southern Realms for decades before settling in the Chultan Peninsula where he terrorized, as black dragons are wont to do, everyone within a hundred miles.

CHULT

This remote peninsula at the far southwestern tip of Faerûn is covered in a dense jungle that hides the ruins of ancient civilizations, tribes of primitive humans, and insidious cells of the serpentine yuan-ti. It's still largely unexplored by Faerûnian humans but occasionally attracts brave or foolish adventurers in search of its hidden treasure. Most of them fall victim to the rampaging dinosaurs that call the jungles home.

ANGELANDER THE STUPID SILVER

Angelander is called "the Stupid Silver" by the red dragon Hephaestus, but the silver dragon is hardly stupid. As regal and benevolent as any silver dragon, Angelander lives in and around the city of Mirabar for decades, commonly taking human form and advising the city's leaders. When Hephaestus appears, Angelander rushes to intercept him. Their duel is a titanic struggle that goes on for days before Angelander finally succumbs to the red dragon's immolating breath.

BLACK DRAGONS

The acid-spitting black dragons live in steaming swamps and jungles where they pounce on their prey from hiding. Evil and ill-tempered, they're also known as "skull dragons" for the tendency of their flesh to pull away from their skulls around their jagged, forward-swept horns.

GODS AND PLANAR DENIZENS

So follows the question of the gods themselves: Are these named entities, in truth, actual beings, or are they manifestations of shared beliefs? Are the dark elves evil because they follow the precepts of the Spider Queen, or is Lolth a culmination of the drow's natural evil conduct?

—Sojourn

GODS OF FAERÛN

There are dozens of gods—good, evil, and neutral—worshiped in Faerûn. Some are identified with primal forces of nature, others are defined by a philosophy or creed. Though the people of Faerûn will invoke the names of any number of gods depending on what favor they hope to receive, a few will devote their lives to one god or goddess, becoming a priest, monk, or paladin in that god's service.

MIELIKKI

Also known as the Forest Queen or Our Lady of the Forest, Mielikki is the sovereign goddess of the natural world. When she chooses to appear to mortals, she takes the form of a beautiful woman with long auburn hair, dressed as a ranger or huntress. She preaches the simple concept that humans and other sentient beings can live in harmony with nature, and her followers forever seek a balance between the wild and the civilized.

Her symbol is the unicorn, and those gentle creatures often serve as her messengers. Clerics of Mielikki are monthly required to perform a ritual called the Song of Trees, in which they call a treant or dryad, then give honor to that creature by performing a few menial tasks for it. Mielikki is a gentle and caring goddess.

TEMPUS

A greater god from the plane of Limbo, Tempus is a god of war and chaos. He's the patron god of warriors throughout the Realms, and his symbol, a flaming silver sword on a field of blood red, is emblazoned on shields, tattooed on arms, and carved into the tombstones of fallen soldiers across Faerûn. When he chooses to show himself to mortals, he appears as a twelve-foot-tall human clad in elaborate plate armor, his face hidden behind a great helm.

UTHGAR

Like Tempus, Uthgar is a god of war, but Uthgar is even more savage than Tempus. He is worshiped by the barbarian tribes of the North. Some say he's Tempus's son, or he may be a mortal barbarian warrior ascended to godhood. Whatever he is, he's the master of a range of eleven animal totems revered by the barbarian tribes. No formal temples to Uthgar exist; instead, he's revered on the field of battle in rites of blood and conquest.

GRUUMSH

The chief god of the orcs lost his eye in an epic duel with the elf god Correllon Larethian. Known forevermore as the One-Eyed God, Gruumsh rules over the orc pantheon with an iron fist, expecting complete obedience from his followers. His shamans advise tribal chiefs and spur them on to conquest and plunder. Gruumsh is only happy when hordes of ravaging orcs are on the march, looting everything in their paths.

DENIER

Denier is a lesser god, the Scribe of Oghma. He sits at the side of the Binder of What is Known and spends his time pouring over the *Metatext*, a tome said to contain all the knowledge in the multiverse. The patron deity of scribes, cartographers, artists, and literary scholars, Denier urges his followers to record everything. Some of the greatest libraries in Faerûn were established in his name.

OGHMA

Called "the Binder of What is Known," Oghma is the god of knowledge. He is thought to be one of the oldest of the gods of Faerûn, having come from some unknown realm not long after the divine sisters Shar and Selûne created Toril. It was Oghma who gave names to the sisters' creations, bringing order to the chaos of the infant world. He remains a patron of esthetics, bards, scholars, librarians, and anyone who seeks knowledge and divine inspiration for new ideas.

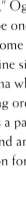

THE ELEVEN TOTEMS OF UTHGAR

The eleven beast totems of Uthgar are the Black Lion, Black Raven, Blue Bear, Elk, Gray Wolf, Great Wyrm, Griffon, Red Tiger, Sky Pony, Tree Ghost, and Thunderbeast. There is a tribe of barbarians in the North for each of these totems, including the Tribe of the Elk, from which Wulfgar hails.

THE TIME OF TROUBLES

In the Year of Shadows (1358 DR) the gods Bane and Myrkul steal the Tablets of Fate from the supreme god—or "overpower"—Ao. Disturbed by what he sees as the gods' greater concern with their petty squabbles with other gods than with the well-being of their mortal followers, the Hidden One forces the gods onto the Prime Material Plane, where they take the forms of their various avatars and come close to ripping the Realms apart in their battles with each other. Some gods grow in power, others are killed or banished, and some mortals ascend to divinity. The war leaves in its wake areas of both wild magic and dead magic, and the face of Toril will never be the same.

MYSTRA

Mystra is the powerful Lady of Mysteries, the goddess of magic who holds the Weave in her capable hands. She is the patron goddess of all wizards and controls the very ebb and flow of magic in Faerûn. Mystra is one of the most active divine powers known, and she often manifests—generally as a beautiful mage—to her followers. Her most ardent worshipers have been elevated to the rank of Chosen. These veritable demigods, including Elminster, Khelben, and the Seven Sisters, are charged with protecting the Art from misuse.

GODS OF THE DWARVES

The dwarves of Faerûn serve a pantheon of gods all their own. These divine dwarves embody all the great virtues of their sturdy, hardworking worshipers. They are as mysterious in their own way as any of the so-called "human gods," but are at the same time more accessible, more like their mortal followers in temperament and action.

MARTHAMMOR DUIN

Generally speaking, dwarves are known as homebodies, rarely if ever leaving the safety of their subterranean halls. But when dwarves venture out into the wide world, they do so with the blessing of Marthammor Duin, the Finder of Trails. Marthammor's clerics tend to be the first to wander off into the world, so they're the most common dwarf clerics encountered in the human cities of the North. Their shrines are open to traveling dwarves, who find solace and aid from the clerics who help to make any dwarf's journey safer.

DUMATHOIN

The patron deity of gem cutters and jewelers, Dumathoin is known as the Keeper of Secrets Under the Mountain. Though at first he was protective of the gems he created and secreted deep in the earth, when the first dwarves began to unearth and cut those gems, Dumathoin was so impressed that he embraced the dwarf gem cutters, reveling in the beautiful creations dwarves fashion from the raw materials he provides.

CLANGEDDIN SILVERBEARD

Dwarf warriors never march to war without the name Clangeddin on their lips. The Lord of the Twin Axes is the dwarf god of battle and the champion of Moradin. His skill at arms is legendary even among the gods, and his martial training and unflagging courage serve as inspiration for every dwarf who's ever picked up a warhammer or axe. He has a strong bond with the other dwarf gods—the so-called Morndinsamman—who also admire his steadfast devotion to their All-Father and his courage in the face of any enemy.

MORADIN

Moradin is the mighty king of the dwarf gods. He can be stern and unforgiving but is a fair and balanced judge and worthy of the loyalty of the other dwarf gods and their mortal followers. The Soul Forger embodies all that dwarves hold dear, and his clerics are expected to help expand the size and influence of the dwarven kingdoms of Faerûn. He was born from the primal stone of the infant multiverse, and his soul burns with the first forge fire ever lit. Moradin is honored by his followers by their constant striving to make their craftsmanship, stonemasonry, and other dwarven work worthy of their All-Father's name.

BERRONAR TRUESILVER

Moradin's wife and the matriarch of the Morndinsamman, Berronar is the patron goddess of healing, home, and hearth. She is almost the polar opposite of Marthammor Duin, in that she encourages dwarves to stay close to home. She preaches the value of family, and would-be parents offer prayers in her name for the children who have been so rare among the dwarves. Though her divine kindness was never brought into question before, many dwarves are beginning to wonder if their low birthrates are a sign of her anger, or worse, her ambivalence.

VERGADAIN

Though he's a loyal member of the Morndinsamman, Vergadain has a darker side that's unusual for the gods of the dwarves. The dwarves of Faerûn are as well-known for their skills as merchants as they are for their craftsmanship, and Vergadain is the Merchant King. His name is never far from the lips of a dwarf who's entering into negotiations, especially with non-dwarves. But Vergadain also encourages trickery that verges on deceit, pushing the dwarves to make the best deals they can. The other dwarf gods see him as a mischievous little brother.

THE QUEEN OF THE DEMONWEB PITS

Mortal servants of the gods of evil are a plague on the face of Faerûn, bringing chaos, murder, war, and hatred. In the same way that their worshipers square off against each other, the gods themselves clash, sometimes in the farthest reaches of the outer planes, and sometimes on the surface of Toril. No force in all the planes is as evil and insidious as Lolth, the Queen of the Demonweb Pits, and her malign servants.

LOLTH

Lolth is a divine power of absolute chaos and the matron of the dark elves. She encourages her worshipers to improve their station by whatever means necessary, including killing each other. She imparts her favor seemingly at random and withdraws it just as capriciously. If she favors a family, that House will prosper, and if she withdraws that favor, they may not know it until they're raided and destroyed by a rival House.

Service to Lolth is the law in Menzoberranzan. There, her priestesses—and only female drow may enter the clergy—hold absolute power, ruling their matriarchal theocracy in the Spider Queen's name. Those priestesses are as cunning, unsympathetic, and merciless as their goddess, who demands sacrifices even from among the drow themselves. Though Lolth can and sometimes does bestow healing spells, her priestesses are encouraged to do nothing but harm to those who show weakness.

Lolth's seat of power is the Demonweb Pits, one of the infinite layers of the hellish Abyss. It is a spider-infested domain of darkness and chaos.

YOCHLOLS

The dreaded handmaidens of Lolth are terrifying creatures that resemble nothing more than a lump of melted wax with fang-lined mouths that thirst for blood. Serving Lolth as messengers and assassins, these fiendish creatures sometimes act as temporary servants to her priestesses. They can communicate via telepathy and have other psionic powers as well, and their bite delivers an insidious poison that weakens their victims, leaving them sickly and lethargic. Yochlols are able to take gaseous form, and in that state they act as conduits between the Prime Material Plane and the Abyss.

VHAERAUN

The Masked God of Night is the god of drow thieves and rogues. His priests are almost entirely male dark elves who passively oppose Lolth's priestesses, insulting them by their very presence. Though Vhaeraun also abides in the Demonweb Pits, his relationship with the Spider Queen is cool at best, and in some places, like Menzoberranzan, his worship is outlawed entirely. He encourages his worshipers to reclaim their place in the World Above, coming up from the Underdark through the shadowy places and infiltrating the surface realms by trickery and deceit.

SELVETARM

Lolth's champion, Selvetarm, is the god of drow warriors, revered by male drow in the service of the matriarchy. He was almost turned away from the path of evil by Eilistraee, but Lolth drove him to battle the demon lord Zanassu. Overwhelmed by Zanassu's evil, Selvetarm's divine soul lay open to Lolth's malignant ministrations, and he has been bound to her ever since. He now exists as a force of vengeance, war, hatred, and violence, in absolute thrall to the Queen of the Demonweb Pits.

KIARANSALEE

The clerics of the Lady of the Dead are a secretive lot, hidden away in smaller communities deep in the Underdark. Their goddess is insane, driven mad centuries ago by the ever-present specter of death. She is the matron of drow necromancers and surrounds herself with the undead. Once a mortal, a powerful necromancer from some distant dimension, she ultimately ascended to godhood. It was Kiaransalee who defeated Orcus, and she continues to work tirelessly to erase all remnants of the demon prince's power on the Abyss. She is a vassal to Lolth, but the two goddesses rarely communicate.

GHAUNADAUR

The most unlikely member of Lolth's court, Ghaunadaur is the god of the amorphous creatures of the Underdark—oozes, slimes, and the like—though his priests are generally drow. His clerics study poisons and acids and are organized in small underground cults lead by a strong, tyrannical high priest. Their god is a brutish thing that revels in the hunting habits of monstrous oozes and jellies, bathing in the misery of things being digested alive.

CREATURES OF THE OUTER PLANES

The Nine Hells and the Abyss are acrawl with horrific creatures that feed on each other in the eternal Blood Wars, while the glabrezu and other creatures of the plane of Gehenna look on in grim amusement. All are servants of evil gods, mortal wizards, demon princes and archdevils. Intelligent and calculating, demons, devils, and their kin are among the most dangerous beings in the vast multiverse.

ULGULU

The barghest whelp Ulgulu and his brother, Kempfana, were exiled to Faerûn until they were old enough and strong enough to return to Gehenna. Vengeful and ill-tempered, Ulgulu feeds off the life-force of mortals, even devouring his own loyal servants when he's made angry enough. Ulgulu has the strength to uproot a tree and tear the stones from the wall of a cave and fully possesses the barghest's innate magical abilities, but he is not quite smart enough to avoid being slain by Drizzt Do'Urden.

KEMPFANA

Like his brother, Ulgulu, Kempfana is a barghest whelp capable of shapechanging into a hideous, wolflike monster. Though he is less temperamental than his brother, Kempfana isn't above occasionally devouring one of his own servants. Kempfana shares one last thing with his brother: he too is eventually killed by Drizzt.

BIZMATEC

The towering glabrezu Bizmatec lives to torment mortals. He is a minion of the balor Errtu, who allows Bizmatec to have his fun with his helpless victims, tearing them limb from limb and consuming them. He has a particular love of strangling his victims in his mighty, crablike claw. Like all glabrezu, Bizmatec is able to call on a myriad of innate magical abilities, including the ability to teleport and to call upon the services of lesser demons.

BARGHESTS

Born in the hellish dimension of Gehenna, barghests are banished as whelps to the Prime Material Plane, where they assume the form of goblins. There they feed on intelligent beings, growing stronger with each kill. Their skin becomes bluer and bluer as they age, and when a barghest's skin is entirely blue, he's likely ready to return to Gehenna as a full-grown adult.

Though they appear to be goblins, they have the ability to change their shapes into a lupine creature akin to a werewolf. Like other outsiders from the Outer Planes, they have a range of innate magical abilities, and though they're but "children" from the point of view of their kind in Gehenna, they are extremely dangerous creatures, terrifying to all but the most powerful of Faerûn's champions.

SERVANTS OF ULGULU

The barghest whelp Ulgulu maintains any number of mortal creatures to serve his every demonic whim.

LAGERBOTTOMS

The rotund hill giant Lagerbottoms serves Ulgulu and his brother, Kempfana, to the best of his limited abilities. Little more than a brutish bully, Lagerbottoms is muscle for the barghest brothers until he meets his fate at the hands of a certain dark elf.

NATHAK

Ultimately devoured by Ulgulu, the barghest he does his best to serve, Nathak is a frail but cunning goblin. He's hardly the first of the barghest's servants to meet this horrible fate, but Nathak loses his life when he brings Ulgulu the bad news that his gnoll tribe had been slaughtered. Barghests aren't above blaming the messenger.

TELSHAZZ

The bloated and toadying solamith Telshazz serves Errtu for a century or longer before finally angering the balor enough that Errtu kills him. Telshazz, who is one of Errtu's messengers, is unable to prevent Al Dimeneira from hurling Crenshinibon across the planes. Hideous, demonic creatures, Telshazz and other solamiths rip off pieces of their own smoldering flesh and hurl them as deadly soulfire missiles. They are cowardly and hunt lesser demons and mortals, whose souls take the form of screaming faces bulging from the solamith's distended stomach.

ERRTU

The mighty balor Errtu seeks total domination of at least one of the infinite layers of the Abyss. He served the circle of liches that created Crenshinibon and became convinced that the Crystal Shard would help him in his plans for conquest. After searching for the shard for centuries, his quest led him to Faerûn, where he allowed Akar Kessell to believe he was under the apprentice mage's control. When Drizzt and his companions wrested the Crystal Shard away from Kessell, they incurred the balor's wrath, making an enemy that is truly to be feared.

A balor is a terrifying creature that ranks just below the demon princes of the Abyss. Errtu shares his kind's malignant intelligence and is possessed of extraordinary magical powers, innate to all balors. He wields a many-tongued whip, which can entangle opponents, and a vorpal sword that releases deadly bursts of lightning.

When he is slain by Drizzt and Guenhwyvar, Errtu's life-force returns to the Abyss, there to remain for a hundred years. The balor vows to take his revenge against Drizzt and even serves as torturer for the Queen of the Demonweb Pits in the hope of finding a way back to the Prime Material Plane. Instead he settles for capturing Drizzt's trusted friend Wulfgar and torturing the barbarian in unspeakable ways for six years in his Abyssal lair.

CRENSHINIBON

From left to right: *First Grandfather Wu, Fetchigrol, Zlan Clervish, Vaeristhelph Rex, Argent Black, Vlad Xil Haerven, Solmé of Gharr*

FIRST GRANDFATHER WU

The first man ever to wield magic on his world of celestial beauty, First Grandfather Wu inadvertently looses a magical plague that kills a billion people.

FETCHIGROL

Fetchigrol was once the shaman of a barbarian tribe from an unnamed plane who sold the souls of the entire population of his world for the power of undeath.

ZLAN CLERVISH

Zlan Clervish is a servant of the dark goddess Shar and one of the first wizards to explore the Shadow Weave, but that knowledge is lost with him and not rediscovered until Shade Enclave escapes the Fall of Netheril by hiding in the Plane of Shadow.

VAERISTHELPH REX

Once the wizard-emperor of an entire world, Vaeristhelph descends into madness when he sacrifices his throne for immortality.

ARGENT BLACK

A being from the depths of the Negative Material Plane, this monstrous lich feeds on darkness and hate.

VLAD XIL HAERVEN

Vlad is the greediest of the seven liches, willing to do anything, however insane, for material wealth.

SOLMÉ OF GHARR

Solmé lives for thousands of years by transferring her life-force into a small child when she grows too old—but her transformation into undeath comes before her last incarnation grows to adulthood.

CREATION AND HISTORY OF THE CRYSTAL SHARD

Crenshinibon is created by a circle of seven liches, powerful undead sorcerers from the far corners of the cosmos. United only by their evil ambitions, the seven liches work their complex ritual and succeed and fail at the same time. Their success comes when the Crystal Shard awakens to its own malignant consciousness, but they fail to adequately protect themselves from Crenshinibon's violent birth spasms. With the balor Errtu looking on, the seven liches are consumed by their own ritual, and Errtu is blasted back into the Abyss by the force of the magical explosion. Awakening under the fire red skies of his home plane, Errtu assumes the Crystal Shard has been destroyed.

But the shard survives. Ultimately a movanic deva by the name of Al Dimeneira tries to capture it, but the shard burns his hands and the celestial throws it across the planes. For millennia it travels the multiverse, possessing hundreds of wielders, some of whom become cruel and powerful tyrants. It eventually comes to rest in Faerûn, in a remote corner of the North, where it lies unfound for countless ages. Finally it calls out to and is discovered by the ambitious apprentice mage Akar Kessell.

POWERS OF THE CRYSTAL SHARD

The Crystal Shard is sentient, though its personality is sublimated by its raw ambition and hunger for chaos and destruction. It feeds off the light of the sun and feels warm and tingling to the touch. When separated from its user the Crystal Shard calls out to sentient creatures for miles around, seeking out someone it can manipulate and control with promises of power and glory. Once it sets its telepathic and empathic tendrils into someone's brain, it cannot be wrested from its wielder by force alone.

The Crystal Shard is capable of sending out a line of fire, and it can give its wielder the power to dominate lesser minds. But its most impressive power is to create the Cryshal-Tirith: towering replicas of itself that act as semi-sentient lairs for the wielder of the Crystal Shard. The power of the wielder to dominate minds is amplified inside a Cryshal-Tirith, making him—or so Crenshinibon would like it to seem—supreme master of his house.

AL DIMENEIRA

Al Dimeneira is a movanic deva, one of the footsoldiers in the eternal war between celestial good and infernal evil. He appears to be a handsome winged elf but is a being of the goodly planes. Al Dimeneira banishes Errtu to the Abyss and attempts to destroy Crenshinibon, but the relic burns him. Despite the demon Telshazz's best efforts, the deva throws the Crystal Shard across the planes in an effort to keep it from Errtu's hands. Al Dimeneira hopes that the relic will be found by someone with the ability, not just the good sense, to destroy it. He certainly couldn't have imagined that that someone would be a dark elf of Menzoberranzan.

REALMS OF THE LEGEND OF DRIZZT

Regis's giant friend, though, continued to shadow their movements. Even as Bruenor, Catti-brie, and the halfling prepared the camp, Drizzt and Guenhwyvar came upon the huge tracks, leading down to a copse of trees less than three hundred yards from the bluff they had chosen as a sight. Now the giant's movements could no longer be dismissed as coincidence, for they had left the Spine of the World far behind, and few giants ever wandered into this civilized region where townsfolk would form militias and hunt them down whenever they were spotted.

—The Silent Blade

FAERÛN

The continent of Faerûn is a landmass of approximately nine and a half million square miles, located mainly in the northern hemisphere of the world of Toril.

Sub-arctic extremes chill its northern reaches, where ice sheets like the Great Glacier dominate the landscape in blinding white. To the south are the equatorial jungles of Chult and the tropical coasts of Halruaa. It's bordered on the west by the Trackless Sea and on the east by the Endless Wastes and the Hordelands that separate it from Kara-Tur.

Faerûn is an open land full of kingdoms and empires, large and small, and scattered city-states and villages struggling to make their way in a landscape that can be unforgiving wilderness one mile and cosmopolitan city the next.

Countless millions of humans, elves, dwarves, halflings, and other sentient beings call Faerûn home. It is a land of magic and intrigue, cruel violence and divine compassion, where gods have ascended and died, and millennia of warfare and conquest have shaped dozens of unique cultures.

1. **Delmarin Island:** This desolate and lonely island is surrounded by reefs inhabited by mysterious fog giants.

2. **Carradoon:** Inhabited by simple shipwrights, the birthplace of the priest Cadderly is a walled town on the shores of Impresk Lake.

3. **The Blade Kingdoms:** A loose collection of city-states that have since fallen into ruins, the Blade Kingdoms were once a realm of spectacular invention and petty warfare.

4. **Thay:** This mysterious realm is ruled by a coalition of wizards who often send agents out into the rest of Faerûn with dark intentions.

5. **Asavir's Channel:** A treacherous but vital sea-lane between the Tethyr Peninsula and the Nelanther Isles that is often harried by pirates.

6. **The Spirit Soaring:** A great cathedral dedicated to the gods Oghma and Denier that is one of the Realms' greatest centers of learning.

THE MOONSHAE ISLES

These rugged, windswept, misty islands are a cold and unforgiving retreat in the northern reaches of the Sea of Swords. Two breeds of humans share what alternates between uneasy truce and all-out warfare. The Northlanders settled from Ruathym and have a long history as raiders, while the Ffolk have lived in the Moonshaes somewhat longer and fancy themselves the more civilized race.

CORMYR

The Kingdom of Cormyr under the rule of King Azoun IV is a shining beacon of civilization and stability that serves as a model for the rest of the Realms. Though hardly without its enemies—most notably the neighboring merchant realm of Sembia and the Zhentarim of Darkhold and Zhentil Keep—Cormyr is a land of peace and prosperity, whose citizens enjoy a high standard of living and personal freedom. The kingdom encompasses all the land between Anauroch and the Dragonmere, from the Marsh of Tun in the west to the Thunder Peaks in the east. Its capital is the city of Suzail.

NELANTHER ISLES

This cluster of islands in the southern Sea of Swords is surrounded by dangerous reefs. Their precarious harborage tends to keep most captains from even trying to land there, but several pirates have charted the reefs and found protected bays and lagoons in which to hide their ships and their treasures. For this simple reason, the Nelanthers have become known as "the Pirate Isles" or, for those worried about confusion with the Inner Sea islands of the same name, "the Pirate Isles of the Sword Coast."

CALIMSHAN

Once a temperate land of mighty forests, Calimshan was settled by humans and halflings in the thrall of the djinni Calim, who established the Calim Caliphates and ruled the region for a thousand years until the efreeti Memnon arrived to challenge his supremacy. What resulted was a magical war known to history as the Era of Skyfire. When the war was over, the once lush forests had become the sun-blasted wastes of the Calim Desert. The humans eventually overthrew their djinni masters and established the city-states of Calimport and Memnon.

MENZOBERRANZAN AND THE UNDERDARK

Never does a star grace this land with a poet's light of twinkling mysteries, nor does the sun send to here its rays of warmth and life. This is the Underdark, the secret world beneath the bustling surface of the Realms, whose sky is a ceiling of heartless stone and whose walls show the gray blandness of death in the torchlight of the foolish surface-dwellers that stumble here. This is not their world, not the world of light. Most who come here uninvited do not return.

—Homeland

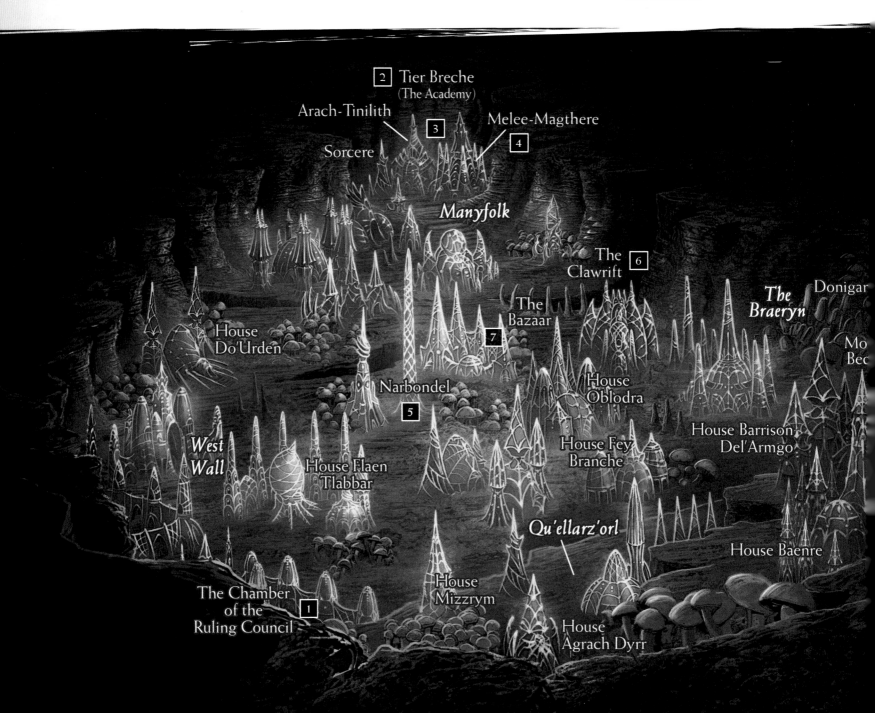

MENZOBERRANZAN, THE CITY OF SPIDERS

Deep in the Underdark below what the surface folk call the North lies a huge natural-chamber home to a sprawling city of dark elves. Menzoberranzan, the City of Spiders, is the birthplace of Drizzt Do'Urden and the center for the worship of the cruel goddess Lolth, the Queen of the Demonweb Pits.

Home to some twenty-thousand drow; thousands more orc, kobold, gnoll, and human slaves; and the occasional illithid, Menzoberranzan is a city of wide, curving avenues passing between huge stalagmite towers into which the great houses of the City of Spiders have been carved. The city possesses a dark, eerie beauty, with intricate carvings highlighted by the shimmering glow of faerie fire that illuminates the city in a ghostly pall of violet, crimson, and azure.

Powerful and heartless priestesses in the service of their demon goddess rule the city with an iron grip, merging the worship of Lolth with the administration of the city to create an unshakable matriarchal theocracy. Menzoberranzan is governed by the matron mothers of the great Houses, the most powerful eight of whom form the ruling council, led by the indomitable First House, House Baenre.

9 The Dark Dominion

Isle of Rothé

1 **The Chamber of the Ruling Council:** The matron mothers convene in this heavily guarded cave to decide the fate of Menzoberranzan.

2 **Tier Breche:** The highest point in the city, guarded by two giant spider statues that animate to protect the Academy

3 **The Academy:** Encompassing Arach-Tinilith, Sorcere, and Melee-Magthere, the Academy is charged with dispensing "justice" in cruel and unforgiving Menzoberranzan.

4 **Melee-Magthere:** Drow warriors train here for ten years and come out deadly, heartless killing machines.

5 **Narbondel:** This stalagmite is heated every evening by Gromph then cools at a steady rate. It is Menzoberranzan's clock.

6 **The Clawrift:** A deep chasm in the shape of a claw. Bregan D'aerthe maintains a secret safehouse in its depths

7 **The Bazaar:** An "open-air" marketplace in which anything—including slaves— can be had for the right price

8 **Donigarten:** A dark freshwater lake whose still waters hide unspeakable creatures and strong undercurrents

9 **The Dark Dominion:** Surrounding Menzoberranzan is maze of treacherous tunnels full of traps, the dangerous magical radiation known as *Faerzress*, and secret meeting places.

ARACH-TINILITH

Housed in a building the shape of a giant spider, Arach-Tinilith is the center of faith for the priestesses of Lolth, and the academy where young drow females are schooled in the demonic practices of their cruel faith. They begin their training at the age of forty, and if they survive the next fifty years of indoctrination, they take their places on the highest rung of the social and political ladder in Menzoberranzan.

The Mistress Mother of Arach-Tinilith is Triel Baenre, who holds court in an office on the highest level, in front of a tapestry that depicts Lolth looming over the sacrifice of a surface elf.

SORCERE

Drow wizards are trained in a tall, gracefully curved and many-spired tower called Sorcere. The masters of Sorcere, led by Gromph Baenre, the Archmage of Menzoberranzan, recruit mostly male drow who begin their three decades of training at the age of twenty-five. The walls of the tower are warded against teleportation, scrying, and other means of magic egress or divination.

HOUSE BAENRE

Located on the enormous ledge called Qu'ellarz'orl, the Baenre compound is made up of twenty gigantic stalagmites and thirty stalactites, is two thousand feet across, and is dominated by a central stalagmite in which the Baenre nobles reside. That central mound is also the location of the Baenre House chapel, a domed shape dominated by an illusion of Lolth that shifts from spider to drow female.

The compound is surrounded by a twenty-foot fence of silvery, clinging webs that are stronger than iron and as thick as a man's arm. Highly trained watchmen guard the perimeter with deadly efficiency.

BLINGDENSTONE, THE CITY OF SPEAKING STONES

Home to a thriving community of deep gnomes, the City of Speaking Stones occupies a series of interconnected caverns about forty-five miles west of Menzoberranzan, in the upper reaches of the Underdark beneath Mithral Hall. The entrance to the city is guarded by a carefully constructed defensive maze designed to bottle up would-be invaders while the svirfneblin attack from cover.

The city itself is remarkable for its natural beauty. The deep gnomes have maintained the organic shape of the stone, but everywhere it's been smoothed into elegant curves. The buildings that dot the various cavern chambers also appear unrefined—little more than piles of rocks—but are in fact carefully and masterfully carved works of art.

1 **The Trader's Grotto:** Blingdenstone's central marketplace houses stalls both temporary and permanent, where the various goods the city lives on are traded.

2 **The Foaming Mug:** This tavern was named in honor of the heraldry of Mithral Hall and caters to dwarf and human travelers to the city.

3 **The House Center:** This is the seat of power in Blingdenstone, where King Schnicktick holds court.

4 **The Speaking Stones:** Ancient menhirs around which the city was built, the Speaking Stones is a holy place that some are beginning to refer to as an "earthnode."

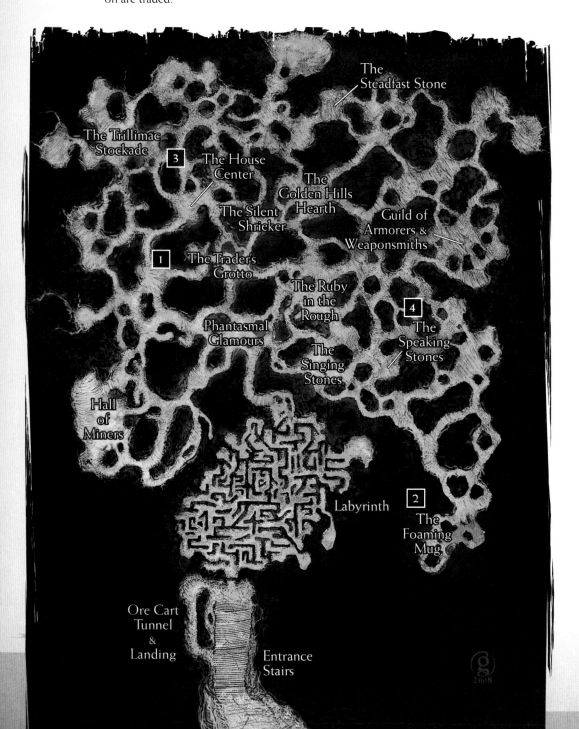

OGREMOCH'S BANE

Though the deep gnomes of Blingdenstone lead a remarkably peaceful life for dwellers in the Underdark, the city is not without dangers of its own. A drifting mist of magical particles invisible to the naked eye, Ogremoch's Bane is named for the lord of evil earth elementals, but its origin is unknown. What is known is that any summoned earth elemental that comes into contact with it is driven into a feral rage, and considerable death, injury, and destruction ensues, forcing the deep gnomes to destroy the once-valued and regal creature.

THE RUBY IN THE ROUGH

A temple devoted to the god Segojan Earthcaller, the Ruby in the Rough is one of Blingdenstone's greatest wonders. Deep below the temple are catacombs that house the mummified remains of the city's honored dead. Above, it is a center of community as much as a center of worship, overseen by the priest Golden Gorger Suntunavick. In keeping with Segojan's wishes, Suntunavick cares for a number of cave badgers, which are loved by the citizens of Blingdenstone but can be dangerous watch animals when the city is invaded.

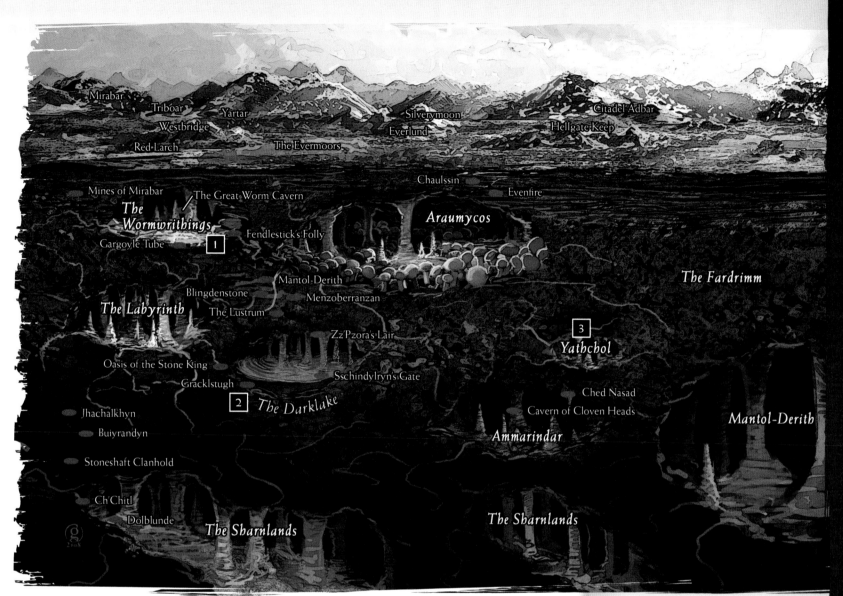

Mirabar
Triboar
Westbridge · Yartar
Red·Larch
The Evermoors
Silverymoon
Everlund
Citadel Adbar
Hellgate Keep

Chaulssin
Eventire
Mines of Mirabar · The Great Worm Cavern
The Wormwrithings
Gargoyle Tube · [1] · Fendlestick's Folly
Araumycos
The Fardrimm
Mantol-Derith
Blingdenstone · Menzoberranzan
The Labyrinth · The Lustrum
[3]
Yathchol
Zz'Pzora's Lair
Oasis of the Stone King
Gracklstugh
Sschindylryn's Gate
Ched Nasad
Cavern of Cloven Heads
[2] *The Darklake*
Jhachalkhyn
Ammarindar
Mantol-Derith
Buiyrandyn
Stoneshaft Clanhold
Ch'Chitl
Dolblunde
The Sharnlands
The Sharnlands

125

[1] **Fendlestick's Folly:** It was in this cave with its fast-moving stream that Drizzt encountered the hermit mage Brister Fendlestick.

[2] **Gracklstugh:** This duergar city lies on the shores of the Darklake and is known as the City of Blades.

[3] **Yathchol:** Yathchol is a cluster of chitine communities where these former slaves of the drow are creating a new society of their own.

THE NORTHDARK

The Northdark is the region of the Underdark that lies below the Silver Marches, from the Sword Coast to the western edge of Anauroch. Great drow cities like Menzoberranzan sit surprisingly close to the cities of deep gnomes and gray dwarves and even pockets of illithids. The Northdark is a mix of every strange thing the Underdark has to offer and is a place both of ancient and elegant, if corrupt, civilizations and wild carnivorous beasts on the prowl for an easy meal.

ARAUMYCOS

Dwarvish for "Great Fungus," Araumycos was first encountered by dwarf miners at the height of Ammarindar, forcing them to abandon productive mines to escape the ever-expanding fungal colony. It is now believed that Araumycos is the largest and oldest living thing on the face of Toril. The fungal colony covers approximately eighty-one thousand square miles and may be at least partially responsible for the lush greenery of the High Forest on the surface above it. Rumors abound that Araumycos is sentient or a manifestation of the myconid god Psilofyr, but no one knows exactly what it is.

ICEWIND DALE AND TEN-TOWNS

Frozen winds blow across the flat strip of tundra north of the Spine of the World, coming in from across the Sea of Moving Ice and freezing everything in their paths, including the hearty barbarians and frontiersmen who call Icewind Dale home. This is a harsh and unforgiving land of fierce tundra yetis, barbarian tribesmen, roaming giants, and ten small towns of tough people from across the Realms who are dedicated to carving a living from the ice and snow. The barbarian tribes follow herds of reindeer, and the people of Ten-Towns fish the clear, frigid waters of their half-frozen lakes while the towering peak of Kelvin's Cairn keeps watch over all.

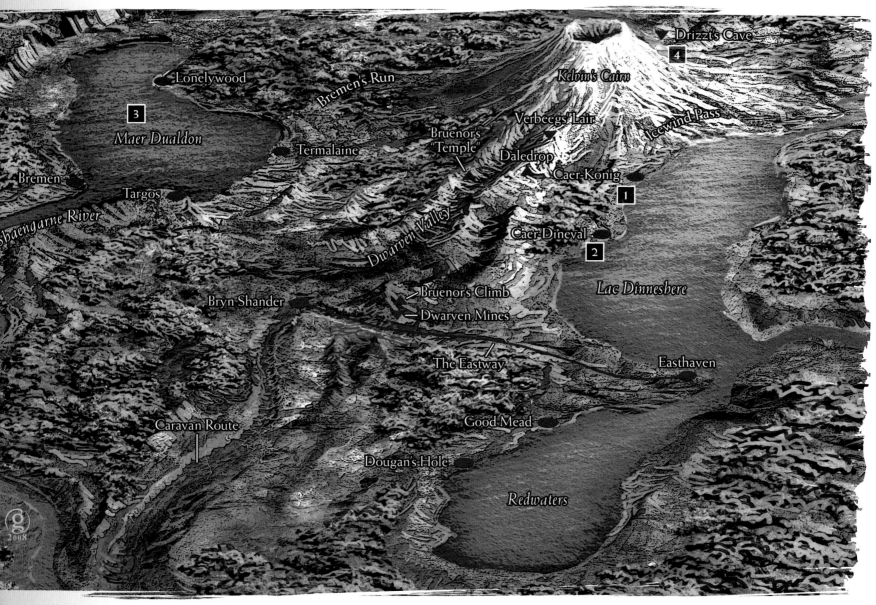

1 Caer-Konig: The town of Caer-Konig agreed to share the fishing rights to Lac Dinneshere with neighboring Caer-Dineval, but that agreement frequently comes under dispute.

2 Caer-Dineval: Caer-Dineval's spokesman, Jensin Brent, greedily guards his town's fishing rights against his counterpart in Caer-Konig.

3 Maer Dualdon: Fished by the four towns that lie on its shores, this cold lake supports a large population of knucklehead trout.

4 Drizzt's Cave: Sparsely furnished with a few skins and minor necessities, Drizzt's cave was a place of safety for a dark elf whose very appearance garnered suspicion.

Verbeegs' Lair

Biggrin and his verbeegs make their home in an abandoned dwarven mine that predates Clan Battlehammer's arrival in Icewind Dale. The verbeegs manage to keep the location of their lair a secret until Akar Kessell's orc scouts happen upon it. When Biggrin joins Kessell's growing army, the wizard uses the lair as a supply depot, and Biggrin is given a magic mirror, located in the Scrying Room, to communicate with Kessell—until Drizzt and Wulfgar put an end to that.

Cryshal-Tirith

Here is a rare look inside the strange tower created by Crenshinibon. Inside, Akar Kessell has arranged a number of magic mirrors that he uses to spy on his enemies and to communicate with his servants. He also maintains a harem and an opulent throne room, both befitting the Tyrant of Icewind Dale.

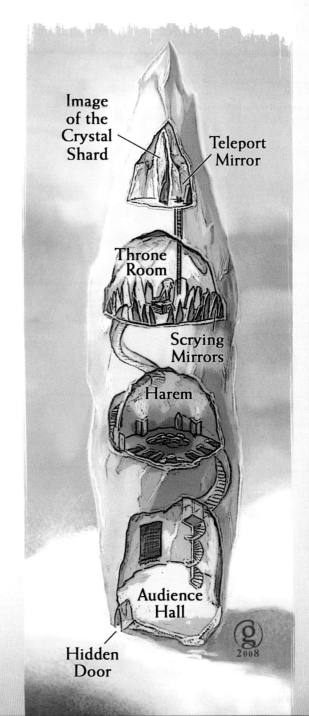

KELVIN'S CAIRN

The snow-capped peak of Kelvin's Cairn rises alone above the frozen tundra of Icewind Dale, the only mountain in a thousand square miles. Because it appears to be a loose collection of boulders piled into a rough pyramid, barbarian legends call it a grave marker, though most likely it is an extinct volcano. Verbeegs make their dens on its rocky slopes, the dwarves of Clan Battlehammer mine a river valley along its south face, and Drizzt found a secluded home in a deep cave on its lonely north face.

BRUENOR'S CLIMB

This stone column four miles south of Kelvin's Cairn has become a place of reflection for Bruenor Battlehammer. It rises only fifteen feet above the ground over the dwarven mines, but from this vantage point Bruenor can look down on the town of Termalaine and the shores of Maer Dualdon.

SHAENGARNE RIVER

The town of Bremen sits on the west bank of the Shaengarne, where the river meets the deep lake Maer Dualdon. Flowing northward from the snowmelt of the Spine of the World, the Shaengarne floods frequently in the spring, but the water level drops in the summer. This is a fairly predictable cycle for the citizens of Bremen, who build as close to the floodplains as they dare, hoping that there's no more winter snow cover on the Spine of the World than normal.

Ten-Towns

The rough-and-tumble pioneers who settle in Icewind Dale are constantly on guard against roaming monsters, raging barbarians, and killing weather. This unforgiving landscape is rich with resources, but it doesn't give up anything easily. The folk of Ten-Towns are a hard lot, but they have come together in close-knit communities where neighbors depend on each other every day for their survival. The towns have attracted their share of rogues, but even these one-time criminals tend to either make themselves a part of the community or face a harsh form of frontier justice—if they aren't smart enough just to head south.

Bryn Shander

The largest of the ten towns, Bryn Shander might more accurately be described as a city, but something in the psyche of the people of Ten-Towns prevents them from using that word. It's a large walled town, at any rate, and being the only one without a fishing fleet, it serves as the primary marketplace for goods from all over the dale and for those imported from the south. It is also the seat of the unified council of spokesmen from the towns, who gather at the Council Hall to discuss matters that affect all of the towns. In times of great emergency, like when hordes of barbarians or humanoids set their sights on Ten-Towns, folk from the communities to the east take shelter in Bryn Shander's walls.

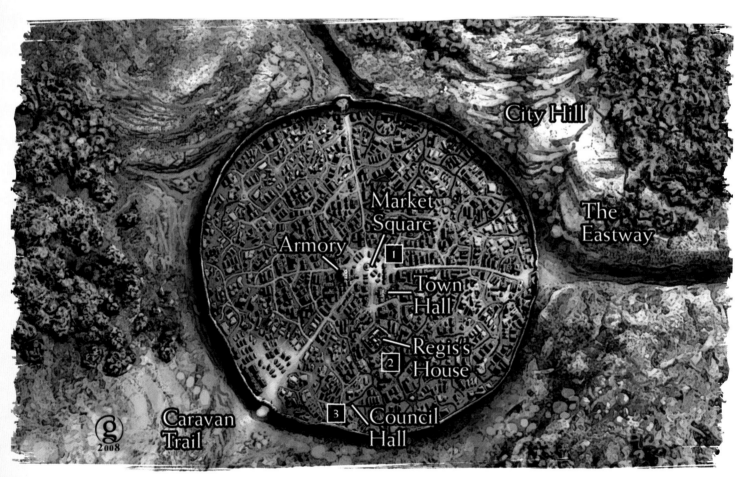

1. **Market Square:** This busy marketplace buzzes with vendors and their customers buying and selling knucklehead trout, scrimshaw, precious vegetables, reindeer meat, and handicrafts.

2. **Regis's House:** This is the house that Spokesman Cassius briefly lent to Regis then took back when he began to doubt the halfling's honesty.

3. **Council Hall:** The spokesmen of all Ten-Towns meet here in often raucous, even violent debates over grudges and policies, wrongs and favors.

TARGOS

The only other one of the Ten-Towns with a defensive wall, Targos is second in size and influence only to Bryn Shander. It is the largest of the fishing towns, and its hundred-boat fleet takes more knucklehead trout from Maer Dualdon than do Bremen, Termalaine, and Lonelywood combined. The city's so-called "Ash Quarter" is a neighborhood where the blackened remains of houses burned by Akar Kessell's third Cryshal-Tirith's beam of searing light set fire to much of the town.

1. **Kemp's House:** The home of the Spokesman of Targos, the suspicious and ornery Kemp.

2. **The Trip and Shuffle:** This rough-and-tumble tavern is not for the faint of heart. The tavernkeeper, Russell, is a disgraced Purple Dragon knight hiding from a death sentence in Cormyr.

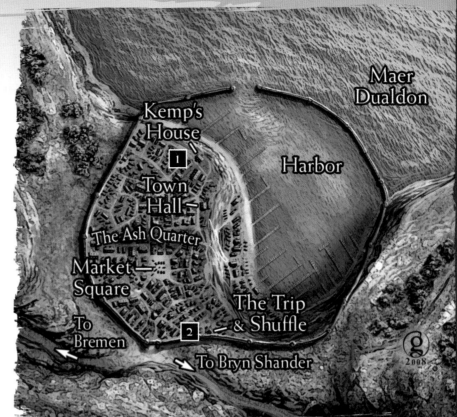

LONELYWOOD

Lonelywood has come to be known as the "Home of the Halfling Hero," referring, of course, to Regis. The halfling served as spokesman for the town, but was succeeded by Muldoon during the Battle of Icewind Dale. A sizeable forest to the east makes Lonelywood one of Ten-Towns' principal suppliers of lumber. It's also known as a first choice for rogues and highwaymen seeking refuge in Icewind Dale—like young Regis himself.

1. **Regis's House:** The halfling still maintains a permanent residence in Lonelywood, though he's since begun to spend more of his time in Mithral Hall.

2. **The Happy Scrimshander:** This little shop provides all the tools of the trade, including exotic ivories, for the many scrimshanders of Lonelywood.

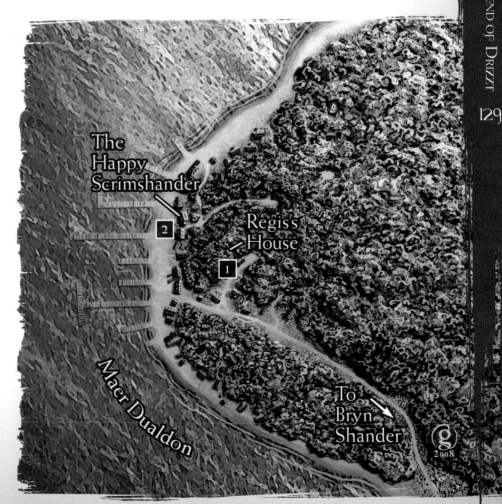

TERMALAINE

When Termalaine is attacked by the barbarians of the Tribe of the Bear during the Battle of Icewind Dale, more than half of the townsfolk take shelter behind the walls of Bryn Shander. They rebuild their quiet, clean town with its wide avenues very quickly after the battle is over. Though the town gets its name from the tourmalines mined by Agorwal, the spelling is a little confused—the townsfolk may not be the most literate people in Faerûn!

1. **Regis Captures deBernezan:** In this alley, the traitor deBernezan met his just fate at the hands of the halfling hero, Regis.

2. **Gem Mine Entrance:** The entrance to the tourmaline mine was long ago sealed when the largely played-out vein started coughing forth some particularly nasty monsters from the Underdark.

EASTHAVEN

It is in the town of Easthaven that Akar Kessell murders his mentor, Morkai the Red, and sets off on the road that leads him to the Crystal Shard and his eventual demise. Thanks to the Eastway, Icewind Dale's best-maintained road, which connects Easthaven and the market town of Bryn Shander, Easthaven is the fastest-growing community in Ten-Towns.

1. **Visiting Dignitaries House:** A house set aside for spokesmen from other towns or other visiting dignitaries, which could be just about anyone save the lowliest wandering trapper or prospector.

2. **The Big Fat Knucklehead:** This out-of-the-way lakeside tavern caters to fishermen. Its proprietor, Flug the Blind, lost one eye to a fishhook and can't see too well out of the other.

BREMEN

Flooding tends to be a difficulty in Bremen, but the citizens have come to understand the signs of approaching high water, and loss of life is extremely rare—at least due to that cause. A number of Bremenites, including their spokesman, Gil Haerngen, search the floodplains for gold nuggets and other treasures washed down from the heights of the Spine of the World. Orc-made weapons and the odd magic item or piece of jewelry—as well as the occasional human skull—have been known to drift down the swollen Shaengarne.

1 Earvin's Treasures: This small shop is run by Earvin Fastul, a wizard from Luskan who settled here after fleeing the Arcane Brotherhood. He identifies and sells the magic trinkets washed down in the floods.

2 Five Tavern Center: A collection of five competing taverns is clustered in the center of town, and fights break out on the circle of gravel between them pretty much every night.

CAER-KONIG

One of the smaller fishing villages of Ten-Towns, Caer-Konig is embroiled in an almost constant dispute with Caer-Dineval over fishing rights to Lac Dinneshere, regardless of the fact that there's every indication that there are plenty of knucklehead trout to go around. Their heavy-handed spokesman, Schermont, isn't making it any easier to find peace, and open warfare is only a minor incident away.

1 Ruined Caer: The ruins of the castle that gives the town its name sit high atop the hill overlooking the harbor.

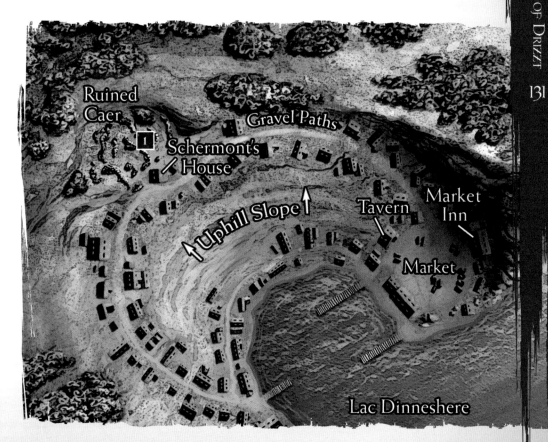

CAER-DINEVAL

The only one of Ten-Towns with a standing castle, the small but reasonably well-maintained caer that gives the town its name is the home of the current spokesman, Jensin Brent. The Dinev family, who originally built the castle in the Year of the Keening Gale (1050 DR), abandoned it less than a decade later in the Year of the Spider's Daughter (1058 DR), when a particularly nasty horde of orcs lay siege to it for so long that the entire population of the surrounding town was killed or ran off. The castle stayed in orc hands for a decade more of orc infighting before the ancestors of the current townsfolk drove off the tattered remnants of the original horde.

1   **The Uphill Climb:** This relatively up-scale tavern caters to traveling merchants with brews brought in from Good Mead and with food from the marketplace in Bryn Shander.

GOOD MEAD

The simple folk of Good Mead are a cheerful lot who tend to keep to themselves. Recently they've begun supplementing their meager fishing profits by exporting the brew that gives the town its name.

1   **Shrine to Tempus:** This small shrine dedicated to the Lord of Battles is the home of an inexperienced young battleguard by the name of Brother Scharamod, who hopes one day to expand the shrine into a proper temple.

DOUGAN'S HOLE

The smallest of the ten towns, Dougan's Hole's population hovers at around a hundred—mostly fishermen who pull knucklehead trout from the cold depths of Redwaters. The lake was originally called Dellon-lune, but it was renamed after a bloody fight between rival fishing boats left corpses to bleed into the water. The current Spokesman of Dougan's Hole is Freya Grynstead, the widow of the previous spokesman who died when his fishing boat floundered in a violent spring storm.

1 The Twenty Stones of Thruun: This huge megalith is a collection of twenty granite slabs forming a perfect triangle. It is named for a long-dead god that may be nothing more than a legend. No one knows who built it or why.

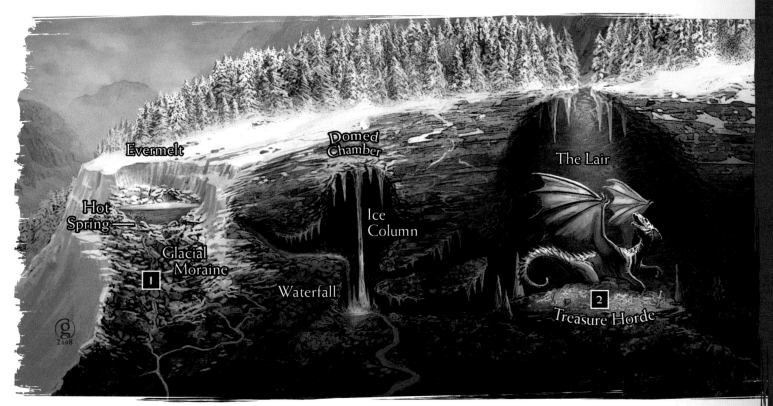

ICINGDEATH'S LAIR

On the frozen expanse of Reghed Glacier, north of Kelvin's Cairn, is the subterranean lair of the mighty white dragon Icingdeath. Above it, the hot spring known by the barbarians as Evermelt provides the wandering tribes with a ready source of fresh water, but few of the tribesmen know that the dragon that inhabited their oldest legends slept under a crust of ice in a cave far below.

The dragon sustained himself on his own treasure, sleeping so long he eventually grew too big to pass out of his cave using the tunnels he'd once climbed in through.

Reghed Glacier forms the eastern border of Icewind Dale and chills the easterly winds the same way the Sea of Moving Ice freezes the winds from the west.

1 Glacial Moraine: A moraine appears as ridges formed of stones and sediment that Reghed Glacier has pushed down and spread beneath it.

2 Treasure Horde: This enormous collection of coins, jewelry, works of art, and magic items is worth a king's ransom, at least. Here Drizzt found the scimitar that forever after would bear the dragon's name.

MITHRAL HALL AND THE SPINE OF THE WORLD

MITHRAL HALL

The ancestral home of Clan Battlehammer, Mithral Hall is named for the hard silvery metal the dwarves mined there for thousands of years until driven off by "dark things in dark holes." After a long and arduous quest, the hall was reclaimed by Bruenor Battlehammer, direct descendant of Gandalug Battlehammer, the First King of Mithral Hall. When Bruenor finally found its hidden entrance, he had to drive off the duergar, who had made it their home, then destroy the shadow dragon Shimmergloom. Neither were easy tasks, but in relatively short order, Bruenor Battlehammer took his rightful place as the Eighth King of Mithral Hall.

The maze of winding corridors under Fourthpeak in a southern spur of the Spine of the World known as the Frost Hills is home to the twenty-five hundred dwarves of Clan Battlehammer and to another two thousand who emigrated from Citadel Adbar with the blessing of King Harbromm. Most of those dwarves inhabit the Undercity, where they forge weapons and sundry items from the mithral, iron, and other metals they mine in the upper reaches of the Underdark.

There are two primary entrances to the hall, both on the southern face of Fourthpeak. A secret entrance opens onto Keeper's Dale, while the main gate is to the east above the River Surbrin. The lowest levels give way to the limitless Underdark, a source of invasion from dark elves, duergar, and others to whom the dwarves of Clan Battlehammer remain constantly alert. The hall is a self-contained city all its own, with shrines to the dwarf gods Moradin, Clangeddin, and Dumathoin, as well as homes, forges, workshops, taverns . . . everything a dwarf needs for a long and happy life.

THE UNDERCITY

This huge chasm is the largest open space in the subterranean city of Mithral Hall, and the vast majority of the dwarves live and work here. The sides of the cavern are shaped in the form of an inverted ziggurat, and the dwarves live on the steps. Their smithies and workshops are on the lowest level, the forge fires giving the whole cavern a homey glow that also fights off the chill of the Underdark. A tall bridge spans the cavern east–to–west, and it's always a busy place with dwarves scurrying about their work at all hours.

GARUMN'S GORGE

Second in size only to the Undercity, Garumn's Gorge is a deep chasm spanned by a newly constructed bridge guarded on each end by stone watchtowers. This is the site of Bruenor's final battle with Shimmergloom, where the king is presumed lost. The waterfall known as Bruenor Falls cascades down the side of the gorge and empties into a cave that in turn feeds the River Surbrin. A little-known cave at the bottom of the gorge leads to the deepest mines east of the Undercity.

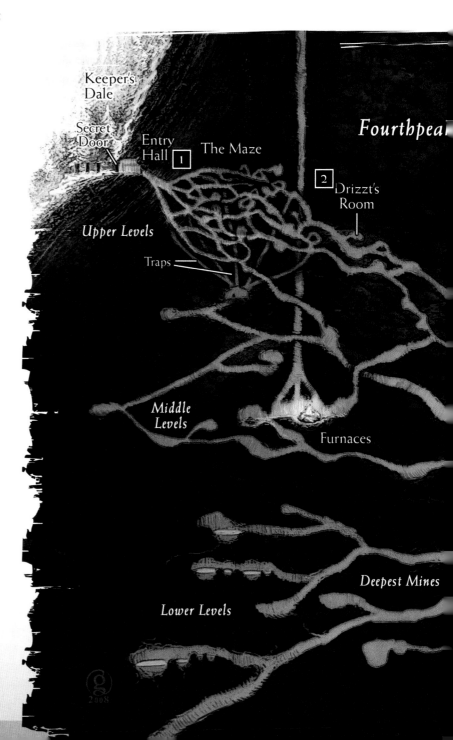

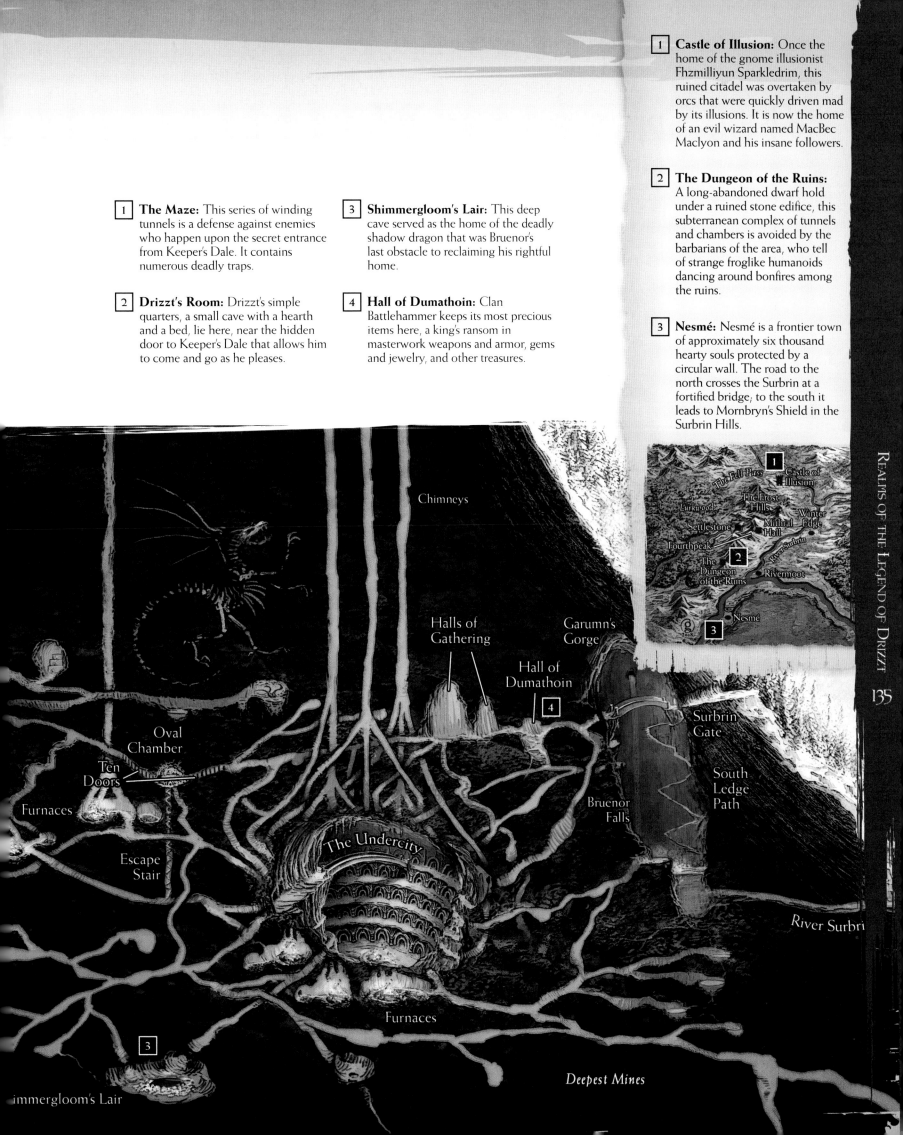

1 The Maze: This series of winding tunnels is a defense against enemies who happen upon the secret entrance from Keeper's Dale. It contains numerous deadly traps.

2 Drizzt's Room: Drizzt's simple quarters, a small cave with a hearth and a bed, lie here, near the hidden door to Keeper's Dale that allows him to come and go as he pleases.

3 Shimmergloom's Lair: This deep cave served as the home of the deadly shadow dragon that was Bruenor's last obstacle to reclaiming his rightful home.

4 Hall of Dumathoin: Clan Battlehammer keeps its most precious items here, a king's ransom in masterwork weapons and armor, gems and jewelry, and other treasures.

1 Castle of Illusion: Once the home of the gnome illusionist Fhzmilliyun Sparkledrim, this ruined citadel was overtaken by orcs that were quickly driven mad by its illusions. It is now the home of an evil wizard named MacBec Maclyon and his insane followers.

2 The Dungeon of the Ruins: A long-abandoned dwarf hold under a ruined stone edifice, this subterranean complex of tunnels and chambers is avoided by the barbarians of the area, who tell of strange froglike humanoids dancing around bonfires among the ruins.

3 Nesmé: Nesmé is a frontier town of approximately six thousand hearty souls protected by a circular wall. The road to the north crosses the Surbrin at a fortified bridge; to the south it leads to Mornbryn's Shield in the Surbrin Hills.

THE SPINE OF THE WORLD

The Spine of the World, also known in some quarters as the Wall, is a range of cold, snow-capped mountains that stretch over six hundred miles from the Sea of Moving Ice in the west to the Ice Spires in the east. It is home to the dwarves of Clan Battlehammer and countless orc tribes, mining operations from the city of Mirabar, and abandoned citadels overrun with monsters, petty fiefdoms, and scattered hamlets. Giants wander its high passes, and pegasus-riding elves patrol its fringes. Most Faerûnians believe the mountains separate the civilized south from the barbarian north, and they aren't necessarily wrong.

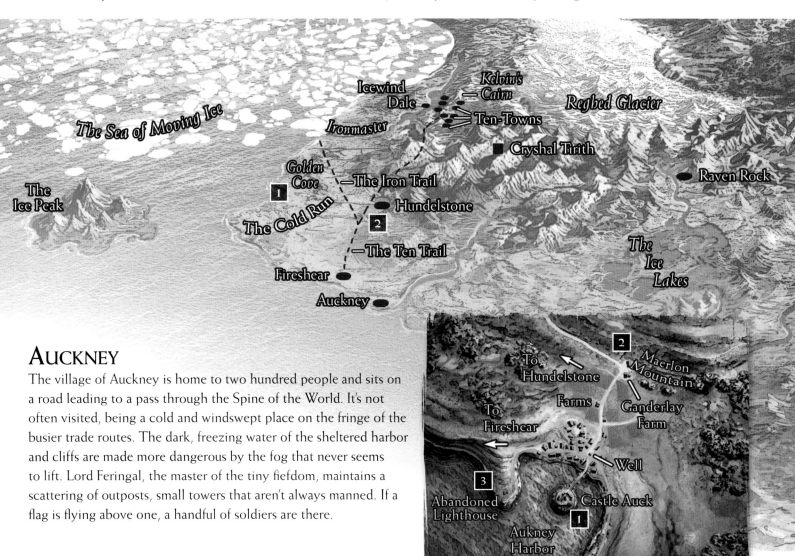

AUCKNEY

The village of Auckney is home to two hundred people and sits on a road leading to a pass through the Spine of the World. It's not often visited, being a cold and windswept place on the fringe of the busier trade routes. The dark, freezing water of the sheltered harbor and cliffs are made more dangerous by the fog that never seems to lift. Lord Feringal, the master of the tiny fiefdom, maintains a scattering of outposts, small towers that aren't always manned. If a flag is flying above one, a handful of soldiers are there.

MIRABAR

This wealthy city on the north end of the Long Road mines the mountains to the north and is a marketplace for the scattered villages, trappers, and prospectors of the central stretches of the Spine of the World. Numerous tunnels and shafts lead into those mines, and a massive undercity, largely inhabited by dwarves, extends deep into the ground beneath the streets.

1. **Castle Auck:** This castle on a tiny island in the harbor was built more than six hundred years ago by the Dorgenast family, but the two fifteen-foot-tall towers and cramped twelve-room house have been the home of the Auckneys, their steward, five more servants, and ten soldiers for more than four centuries.

2. **Ganderlay Farm:** Typical of the subsistence-level farms that feed the village of Auckney, the Ganderlay family scratches out a meager living on the steep side of Maerlon Mountain.

3. **Abandoned Lighthouse:** No one currently alive in Auckney remembers this lighthouse as anything but a crumbling ruin, but sometimes, if the wind is coming from the west, people say they can hear a woman screaming from somewhere inside the leaning tower.

VALLEY OF KHEDRUN

The legendary dwarf prospector Khedrun is said to have discovered the greatest cache of gems the world has ever seen. He went on to carve a place in the Spine of the World for his brother dwarves, using only his axe. The valley is now thought to be the location of the legendary Gauntlgrym.

SHINING WHITE

An ancient barbarian burial cairn, Shining White gets its name from the vales of blinding white soil where the barbarians have cut through the permafrost to the chalk layer, as well as from the bright white marble menhirs that mark it as a sacred place.

1 **Golden Cove:** This series of sea caves houses Sheila Kree's pirate crew and the ogres of Clan Thump.

2 **Hundelstone:** Twelve hundred gnomes and humans call this simple trade town home.

3 **The Endless Ice Sea:** This enormous glacier remains largely unexplored, though rumors and legends of treasure troves and places of magic abound.

4 **Gate:** The beholder Zythalarlr and his bugbears guard the portal at the heart of this ancient ruin.

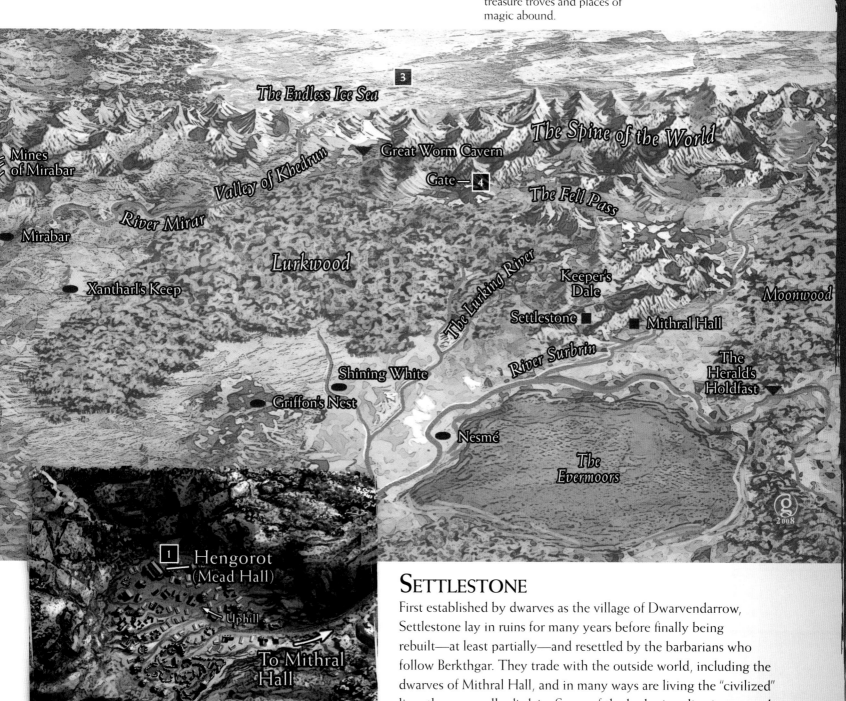

SETTLESTONE

First established by dwarves as the village of Dwarvendarrow, Settlestone lay in ruins for many years before finally being rebuilt—at least partially—and resettled by the barbarians who follow Berkthgar. They trade with the outside world, including the dwarves of Mithral Hall, and in many ways are living the "civilized" lives they normally disdain. Some of the barbarians live in restored stone buildings, but at least as many live in tents. Settlestone is a cold, windy place, boxed in on three sides by tall mountains.

1 **Hengorot:** The mead hall, or *Hengorot*, is the center of the barbarian camps of Icewind Dale and the Spine of the World. It's a huge deerskin tent, big enough to seat as many as four hundred barbarians at its long tables.

THE NORTH

In many ways the North—known variably as the Silver Marches, the Savage North, the Savage Frontier, or by other less charming epithets—is a territory marked by extremes. Barbarians and savage orcs raid their neighbors with inhuman violence, while cosmopolitan cities like Silverymoon are shining jewels of peace and civilization. It is a land where adventurers seek their fortunes side-by-side with prospectors, trappers, bounty hunters, and sellswords. The winters are long and cold, and everywhere are the threats of strange creatures, carnivorous animals, and even slavers coming up from the Underdark to snatch the unwary into a life of servitude in the dark cities of the drow. But the North is also the home of thousands of people determined to civilize the uncivilized and tame the untamed.

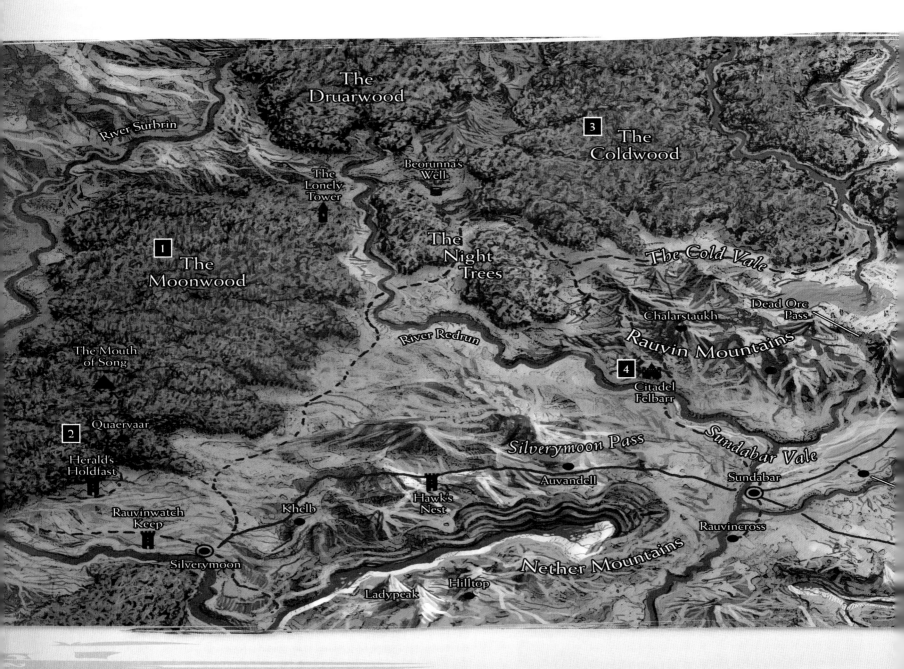

BEORUNNA'S WELL

This ancient ancestor mound and barbarian village is named in honor of the legendary hero Beorunna, the mythical father of Uthgar. The five hundred members of the Black Lion tribe who call it home live in modest houses surrounding the deep pit into which the ancestral mound sank when Beorunna destroyed the demon Zukothoth. Unspeakable horrors of the Underdark now lurk at the bottom of that pit, and the barbarians fear its depths as much as they revere its history.

DEAD ORC PASS

Drizzt Do'Urden first emerges from the Underdark onto the World Above through a cave in this lonely pass deep in the heart of the Savage North. Though it's a ready passage between Citadel Adbar and the trade city of Sundabar, most caravans continue to take the longer road route around the Rauvin Mountains to avoid the many orcs that call this place home and lie in wait for anyone brave or stupid enough to pass through it.

SUNDABAR

Sundabar is a major walled city originally constructed by dwarves, but it now boasts a population of nearly forty thousand, almost all of whom are human. The Master of Sundabar, Helm Dwarf-friend, is a wise and charismatic leader, and the city is a hub of trade, collecting ores from the mines of Citadel Adbar and the Underdark dwarves of Fardrimm as well as goods from Everlund, Silverymoon, and throughout the North. It's a prosperous and peaceful city, protected by sellswords including Helm Dwarf-friend's own Bloodaxe Mercenary Company.

1. **The Moonwood:** The depths of this mighty forest are places of mystery, where legends tell of crumbling ruins and strange rites, all protected by elves wielding extraordinary magic.

2. **Quaervaar:** What started as a simple logging camp has grown to a town of almost eight hundred humans and half-elves who cull the trees of the Moonwood with great care and reverence.

3. **The Coldwood:** Once the domain of wild elves, the Coldwood is now the territory of wandering ettins and the occasional wizard seeking a quiet place to pursue his arcane research.

4. **Citadel Felbarr:** A dwarven citadel ruled by the powerful and righteous King Emerus Warcrown, Felbarr was only recently retaken from a band of orcs who had held it as the Citadel of Many-Arrows.

CITADEL ADBAR

The most powerful of the dwarven citadels of the North, Citadel Adbar is ruled by the mighty King Harbromm. Harbromm is a close—but always fiercely independent—ally of Lady Alustriel of Silverymoon and King Bruenor of Mithral Hall. It is only through Harbromm's aid that Bruenor is able to retake Mithral Hall, and more than two thousand Adbar dwarves migrated there. Mithral Hall and Citadel Adbar share more than a dwarf's pride and a love of mining—they share families.

1. **The Caravan Door:** This series of massive iron portals seals off the lower reaches of the citadel from the Underdark entrances to the Fardrimm and other parts of fallen Delzoun.

2. **Dragonspikes:** The tall towers of the upper levels of the citadel are protected from attacking dragons by a nasty series of needle-sharp spikes.

CITIES OF THE SWORD COAST

The Sword Coast is where the vast Trackless Sea meets the western coast of Faerûn. The sea's warm waters are home to merchants and pirates who ply the busy sea lanes from the city of Luskan in the north, south all the way past Athkatla to Calimport and beyond. Some of the biggest and wealthiest cities on all of Toril lie along the rocky shores of the Sword Coast, including the Jewel of the Realms, the mighty City of Splendors: Waterdeep.

1 **Neverwinter Wood:** This large forest of oak and birch trees is a beautiful and restful spot in the daylight but oppressive and unsettling at night.

2 **The Trade Way:** The Trade Way is a long stretch of well-maintained road—a vital caravan route between Waterdeep and the southern Heartlands.

3 **Orlumbor:** A rocky island with treacherous harborage, Orlumbor is the home of a small city-state that few take the time to visit.

4 **Athkatla:** This southern Sword Coast city is the capital of the realm of Amn, where commerce is the law of the land.

TOWER OF TWILIGHT

The Tower of Twilight is the creation of the wizard Malchor Harpell. It exists in another dimension, showing itself only briefly in the twilight hours. The door remains in place, though—but only for those who know how to find it. When the tower appears on the Prime Material Plane, it is a beautiful structure of emerald green stone topped with two twisted, hornlike spires. A circular ramp leads from the stable on the ground floor through Malchor's residence up to cramped chambers that the mage uses for meditation and divination.

1 **Malchor's Museum:** In this torchlit chamber the master of the tower maintains a collection of fine works of art, both mundane and magical, that rivals any private collection in Faerûn.

2 **Invisible Bridge:** The tower is surrounded by a pond crossed by a bridge that is usually invisible but can glow with an enchanted green light.

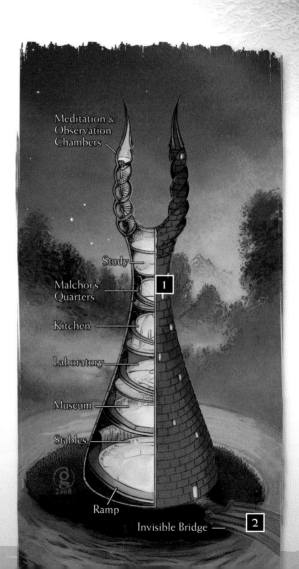

Meditation & Observation Chambers

Study

Malchor's Quarters — 1

Kitchen

Laboratory

Museum

Stables

Ramp

Invisible Bridge — 2

LONGSADDLE

The village of Longsaddle is an unassuming rural community of simple farming folk who take a certain pride in their claim to be "between everywhere." The village is more or less halfway between Luskan and Silverymoon and halfway between Mirabar and Waterdeep, but why someone might be proud of that is something only a citizen of Longsaddle might be able to tell you.

What makes Longsaddle significant to outsiders is the family of wizards who make their home on a hill that bears their name just outside the village limits. The Harpells live and work in the sprawling Ivy Mansion, a trio of buildings that tower over Longsaddle. Two of the buildings appear to be simple farmhouses, but the third is truly unique. The central house was built with odd angles, frequent niches, and dozens upon dozens of turrets and spires—no two of which are exactly alike.

A fence of invisible magical force surrounds the mansion, with the quirky touch of having fence posts painted onto it. This is only one of the many oddities one might encounter on a visit to the Ivy Mansion. A bridge you traverse by walking on the underside, a barn full of experimental animals—twisted creations of a disturbed mind—and a plethora of magical wards and illusions make the Ivy Mansion a veritable wonderland that is both beautiful and dangerous.

Inside, the Harpells maintain a tavern of their own they call the Fuzzy Quarterstaff. In this enormous circular room, the hub of the Ivy Mansion, a wand-wielding wizard conducts an invisible orchestra, and guests order drinks and meals from a centerpiece in the form of a fist-sized green gem on every table. The "waiters" are blue floating disks of magical energy.

CONYBERRY

This tiny village on the edge of the Neverwinter Wood is home to only a few dozen families, mostly farmers who sell their goods in neighboring Triboar. But just past the edge of the woods, in a dark cave just barely large enough for a man to crawl into, hidden by a stand of tall trees, and protected by illusions and mirrors, lies the cave of the restless spirit the villagers call Agatha—a banshee that guards an ancient and valuable treasure.

MERE OF DEAD MEN

This dense and treacherous swamp is dotted with crumbling ruins inhabited by the restless dead. Fearless adventurers from all over the Realms have tried their luck in the Mere of Dead Men, and no small number of them are still there, wandering the oppressive, stinking bogs as shambling corpses animated by fell necromancy

CANDLEKEEP

A huge and imposing fortress rising above the rocky cliffs west of the town of Beregost, Candlekeep is a massive library widely considered to be the greatest collection of books, scrolls, loregems, and other historical artifacts spanning the whole of recorded history on Toril. It is well guarded by priests of Oghma, and admission to its secretive inner bailey, let alone to the libraries themselves, is strictly limited.

LUSKAN

The walled port city of Luskan lies at the mouth of the fast-moving River Mirar and is home to some fifteen thousand people—mostly humans. Barely a tenth of the size of Waterdeep, it's not quite as important a destination, but Luskan's far northerly location makes it the perfect gateway for ore and other goods from the Spine of the World and beyond—including scrimshaw from Ten-Towns.

The City of Sails is a place where sailors try to get back to their ships before it gets too dark and are loath to be caught out on the streets alone after having had too much to drink. Thieves prowl the quayside, ambushing their victims from behind the piles of broken crates and refuse that line the dockside alleys, which are further hidden by the fog that rolls in from the sea in the evening. Halflings and anyone who appears small and weak are favorite victims, but even soldiers avoid the docks at night.

The overwhelming majority of Luskan's citizens are human, and life in the tough and unforgiving city has made them more than a little difficult. They tend to come off as tense, even paranoid, and are prejudiced against non-humans of any kind—so much so that few non-humans make it through the well-guarded gates in the first place. For the most part, only merchants are welcome.

Though the city is dominated by two- and three-story buildings, the Hosttower of the Arcane rises high above the skyline from an island at the river's mouth. This school for wizards is among the most highly respected in all the Realms, but it has a dark side too.

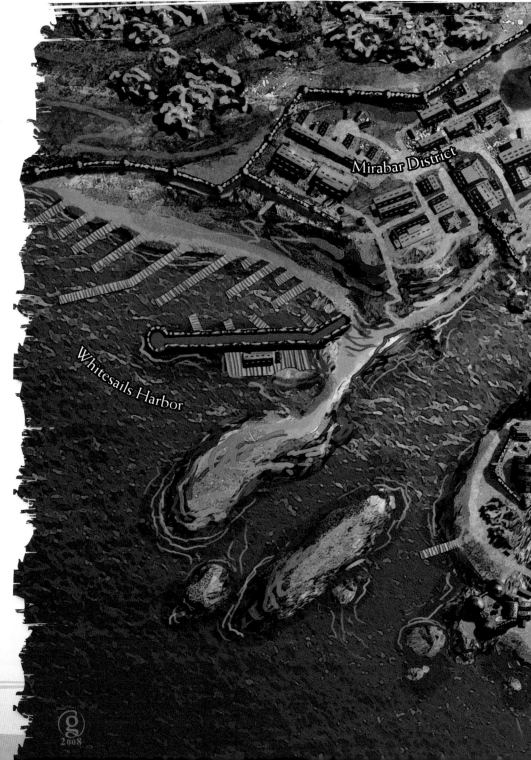

1 North Gate: This huge, iron-bound door has a square tower on each side and is backed by a portcullis. Soldiers led by the Nightkeeper of the North Gate guard the entrance to the city, armed with spears and crossbows. In the winter they're issued fur caps.

2 Illusk Ruins: Scattered remnants of the long-lost city of Illusk stand as crumbled walls and moss-grown statues, haunted by dangerous undead creatures.

3 Prisoners' Carnival: This gruesome, blood-spattered platform is the site of horrifying public torture and executions, carried out by sadistic half-orc gaolers.

4 Rat Alley: This already narrow alley is further crowded by discarded crates and other refuse, and is lined on both sides by low storehouses and thieves in hiding.

THE HOSTTOWER OF THE ARCANE

This towering citadel resembles a four-limbed tree and houses a college of wizards dominated by the mysterious Arcane Brotherhood. The building itself radiates a palpable aura of magic that many find unsettling, and it's not uncommon for the people of Luskan to go tendays without chancing a glance up at it. It's made of solid stone, obviously created by powerful spells. What happens inside is kept a closely guarded secret, but it's been said that every apprentice is given his own alchemical laboratory and meditation chamber.

THE CUTLASS

This popular seaside tavern on Half-Moon Street is marked, above the door, by a weather-beaten, faded sign that few of its patrons—sailors, rogues, and dock rats all—can actually read. The tavernkeeper, Arumn Gardpeck, keeps the place as peaceful as possible, usually by hiring the biggest, brawniest men he can find to work the door. The main room stinks of stale air and old pipeweed, and up a short flight of stairs are a few rooms where, for a price, some local women entertain the customers.

WATERDEEP

The City of Splendors is certainly the greatest of the Sword Coast cities and perhaps the greatest city on the face of Toril. It's home to as many as two million people, though an accurate census is all but impossible since so many come and go, visiting the open city to trade and otherwise seek fame and fortune. Waterdeep is a stable and generally peaceful city, where the rule of law is enforced by a huge and well-equipped watch further backed up by some of the most powerful personalities in the Realms, including Khelben "Blackstaff" Arunsun, Waterdeep's defacto archmage, and the heroic paladin Piergeiron.

Still, there are parts of Waterdeep that can be dangerous for the unwary, and the rough-and-tumble Dock Ward is one of those parts. The detailed map shows the area around Dock Street, where *Sea Sprite* finds harborage.

1 **Dock Street:** Running the length of Waterdeep Harbor, this infamous lane is always crowded with strangers to the city just off the many ships that dock there.

2 **Seaswealth Hall:** This large but unassuming building is the guildhall of the Fishmonger's Fellowship, which controls the city's lucrative open-air fish markets.

3 **Red Sails Warehouse:** Cheap and secure storage in the form of coffin-sized lockboxes can be rented here for a reasonable price—the gods only know what treasures might be secreted there

4 **Warm Beds:** Shalath Lythryn runs this inviting inn, where heated stones are used to warm guest's beds, and peace and quiet is the order of the day.

WATERDEEP HARBOR

This busy harbor is protected by enormous gated sea walls above the surface and by a cadre of merfolk beneath it. It is known all over the world as the safest of harbors, with the finest repair facilities for ships from across Toril and with everything a merchant captain needs—from storehouses and marketplaces to myriad inns, festhalls, and taverns for the entertainment of his crew.

THE MERMAID'S ARMS

This loud and raucous dockside tavern and festhall is a favorite of *Sea Sprite*'s crew and one of the few places the pirate hunters are allowed to fully relax. The barmaids tend to be on the surly side, but other women who frequent the establishment are rather more welcoming—at least for a little while, and for a few gold pieces. The tavern is run by Calathia Frost, a smart and street-savvy woman who values the privacy and safety of her guests.

BALDUR'S GATE

The port city of Baldur's Gate technically isn't even on the Sword Coast but lies some miles inland on the wide and deep River Chionthar. Still, it's a busy Sword Coast port for captains who don't mind coming a bit upriver. The walled city is divided into two major districts: the lower city is nearer the riverside docks, and the upper city is uphill toward the walls. The busy harbor is overseen by a harbormaster, who resides in a small shack near the piers and is perhaps a little over-protective, as the harbor is closed after sunset, and no ships are allowed to tie up at the piers after dark. As such, most mornings dawn with at least half a dozen ships awaiting a berth, anchored in the wide river.

1 **The High Hall:** This is the palace of the four grand dukes who rule Baldur's Gate—a place surprisingly accessible to all citizens.

2 **Seatower of Balduran:** This defensive citadel on an island in the harbor is named for the legendary explorer Balduran, a foreshortened version of which names the city itself.

3 **Sorcerous Sundries:** A well-stocked curio shop that caters to wizards of every stripe, Sorcerous Sundries sells everything from arcane and exotic material components to fully functional magic items.

4 **The Counting House:** Coins, gems, and valuables from all over Toril are exchanged at this thriving moneylender, who holds marks over all the finest people in the Gate.

CALIMPORT

The largest city in all of Faerûn, Calimport is a sprawling metropolis that is the absolute center for trade and commerce in the southern Realms. It is a place of sharp distinctions, where the rich are richer and the poor are poorer than anywhere in Faerûn. The towering white marble spires of the wealthy pashas mingle with the tattered tents and crumbling shanties of the poor. An alarmingly huge percentage of the population lives a life of bare subsistence and inhabits whatever corner of the streets they can claim. The city's streets reek with human and animal waste, and in some places even the foul odor of decaying bodies left in ditches, unburied and unmourned. At the same time lofty temples and majestic palaces stretch skyward, and the pashas live in utter luxury, enjoying a constant influx of goods and gold from across Toril.

In contrast to the cities of the northern Sword Coast, the streets of Calimport really come alive after sundown, when the scorching heat of the day succumbs to the cool breezes of the desert night. Beggars line every winding thoroughfare and practically choke the marketplaces, where they compete for the attention of the millions of people who've come to the capital city of Calimport to live and work.

1 **Rogues' Circle:** This cul-de-sac just north of Pook's palace is lined with iron grates that lead into the sewers—grates that appear to be intended to keep things inside from getting out.

2 **The Spitting Camel:** This safe and reasonably priced inn just off Rogues' Circle is run by a nervous man who doesn't do much to make his guests feel at home.

3 **Avenue Paradise:** Avenue Paradise is one of hundreds of streets in Calimport where strange varieties of pipeweed, stolen goods of all sorts, and temporary companionship can be had for the right price.

4 **The Coiled Snake:** This inexpensive inn's rooms are tiny, hot, and noisy, and guests share them with a variety of insects and rodents—a pretty typical establishment for most of Calimport.

Tomnoddy's Inn

Temple and Learning Quarter

Plaza of Divine Truth

Trade Way

The Pasha's Palace

Armada Barracks

Calimport Armada

The Shining Sea

Pasha
Basadoni's
House

Rogues
Circle

The
Spitting Camel

2

Pasha
Pook's
Palace

1

Market
Quarter

Craft Quarter

The Coiled Snake

4

Dock Quarter

Avenue
Paradise

The
Copper
Ante

3

Shipyard

PASHA POOK'S PALACE

The home of this wealthy pasha is also
the headquarters of the largest and most
dangerous thieves' guild in Calimport.
Here, Pook can relax in his harem one
moment and order the torture of a rival
in the Cells of Nine the next. Unlike the
imposing white marble facades of his
fellow pashas, Pook's residence appears
to be a nondescript brown storehouse,
but inside it is a sort of fairyland of mad
excess. Even his guards wear the guise
of beggars—his neighbors have no idea
that Pook is one of the wealthiest men in
the city.

THE CELLS OF NINE

Deep in the bowels of the thieves'
guild of Pasha Pook lies a chamber of
unspeakable horrors in which Pook
tortures rival thieves and anyone else
who stands in his way. Only one of the
nine cells, the one in the center, is left
for his hapless prisoners. The other eight
surrounding it are home to large hunting
cats, including a rare white lion, captured
and imported from the four corners of
Toril. The cats are allowed to claw and
bite at the prisoners, and the only place
that's out of reach of the cats is the exact
center of the ninth cell.

THE COPPER ANTE

This large and crowded gambling hall,
festhall, and pipeweed den is run by the
halfling Dwahvel Tiggerwillies. Halflings
staff the gaming tables and festhall
alike, so it's a place of peculiar tastes,
catering to the wealthy and adventurous.
Dwahvel prides herself on the quality
of her Thayan brown pipeweed, on the
beauty of her halfling ladies, and on
the fairness (as far as you know) of her
games. Though she's not so proud of
her wererat brother, Dondon, whom she
keeps chained in a back room.

MONSTERS OF THE LEGEND OF DRIZZT

Graul had been chieftain for many years, an unusually long tenure for the chaotic orcs. The big orc had survived by taking no chances, and Graul meant to take none now. A dark elf could usurp the leadership of the tribe, a position Graul coveted dearly. This, Graul would not permit. Two orc patrols slipped out of dark holes shortly thereafter, with explicit orders to kill the drow.

—Sojourn

CREATURES OF THE UNDERDARK

Though it would be impossible to list all the myriad things that scuttle about in the Stygian blackness of the Underdark, hungrily reaching out for prey or hiding from a bigger dweller in darkness, here are some of the most dangerous encountered by Drizzt.

CAVE FISHERS

These seven-foot-long arachnids live in the dark corners of the Underdark, where they hide in the tops of caves and tunnels. They hang long strands of strong webbing to snare passing creatures, including humans and drow, though they prefer bats and other flying creatures of the Underdark. Once a victim is ensnared in these sticky webs, cave fishers use their powerful, lobsterlike claws to drag their prey up into their hungry mouths. In a pinch they'll fire strands of webbing at creatures who have evaded their trap lines, dragging them back like a man with a fishing line—hence their name, cave fishers. Though they're often encountered on their own, they also live in clusters of up to four individuals, who cooperate in trapping, killing, and eating. With the ability to drag as much as four hundred pounds up with their trap lines, few creatures are big enough to be safe from cave fishers.

DIATRYMA

The diatryma is an Underdark cousin of the axebeak. A little smaller than their surface ancestors, these flightless birds grow to between four and six feet, while the axebeak can reach seven feet tall. Diatrymas are also a little slower on their feet than the fast-running axebeaks but are more nimble. To make up for eyes that have grown less sensitive in the Underdark, they have developed a more acute sense of smell than their surface-dwelling cousins and tend to have an even nastier disposition.

DIRE CORBIES

The dire corby is a remote ancestor of a surface bird that migrated into the Underdark and was mutated in strange ways. Having lost the power of flight, their wings eventually developed into muscular arms, though they retained the taloned feet of their progenitors. Covered in black feathers, they're difficult to see in the darkness, where they lie in wait then swarm and claw their prey in flocks of up to a dozen individuals. Though feral and primitive, they possess a rudimentary intelligence. Their call sounds something like the word "doom," but they may not actually be speaking Common. That might be just an unsettling coincidence. . . .

GRUBBERS AND BARUCHIES

Grubbers are enormous caterpillars, as big around as ten feet in diameter and seven or eight times that long. Their slimy, pale gray bodies are lined with rows of tiny little feet with sharp claws that they use to burrow through solid rock, leaving tunnels snaking through the bedrock behind them. Though they're temperamental, territorial creatures, their mouths are too small to pose a threat to something as large as a human, and they're herbivores besides, feeding on molds and fungus. The baruchie, or so-called "crimson spitter," is their favorite delicacy. Baruchies are fungal colonies that grow wild in the Underdark, emitting a soft red glow. Stepping on it or otherwise disturbing it causes the baruchie to spit out a choking cloud of spores.

MYCONIDS

Also known simply as "fungus men," myconids actually have no gender and reproduce, like other fungus, through spores. Shy and xenophobic creatures, their communities, which are home to as many as two hundred myconids, are found in the darker, more remote regions of the Underdark. They avoid contact with other sentient species as best they can and will fight to protect their homes.

As they grow, they're able to use their spores for various purposes, including telepathic communication and asexual reproduction. Their communities are made up of collections of "circles," with each circle consisting of twenty individuals. The largest member of the community assumes the role of king and practices an enigmatic form of fungal alchemy.

KOBOLDS

These cruel and violent little humanoids look like a cross between a dog and a lizard that is walking on its hind legs. Their hairless bodies are covered in coarse scales, and they stink like a wet dog. Found throughout the Underdark, they live in tribal groups of up to six hundred or more but are really only dangerous in large numbers. Not terribly physically strong or intelligent, they're considered a nuisance by most of their neighbors and often wind up as slaves for more powerful creatures, including the drow. The dark elves of Menzoberranzan breed kobold slaves in the Clawrift and use them as frontline troops, not particularly interested in how many might perish in an effort to overwhelm an enemy. The kobolds breed fast enough that fallen slaves are easily replenished.

THOQQUA

The svirfneblin measure distance by "how the rockworm burrows." Known interchangeably as rockworms or in Undercommon, *thoqqua*, these beasts of elemental earth and fire burrow through solid stone by melting it. Their cone-shaped heads burn red-orange, and the rest of their bodies are so hot that touching one can scald a human. Violent and angry hunters, thoqqua hurl themselves at their prey in an effort to burn them to death. They're only a foot in diameter and four or five times that in length, but they are dangerous creatures nonetheless.

DEEP ROTHÉ

The deep rothé are closely related to the rothé that are kept by surface-dwelling farmers throughout the North. These Underdark herd animals are a little smaller, standing three or four feet at the shoulder. The strangest difference, though, is the deep rothé's ability to conjure magical lights that they use to communicate simple concepts within a herd. The deep rothé are also inured to the harmful effects of fungus and mold. It's believed that both of these characteristics were intentionally bred into the animals by drow wizards. The dark elves are fond of rothé meat, and few drow communities are without a deep rothé herd. Those who've tasted both maintain that the meat of the deep rothé is much more tender and less gamey than that of the surface animal.

SPIDERS

The Underdark is acrawl with a staggering number of different kinds of spiders, from harmless little creatures the size of a speck of dust to ghastly eight-legged behemoths that make the surrounding stone quiver with their every step. Some possess crippling or deadly venom, while others just eat their prey alive.

VELSHARESS ORBB

Similar to, but much more dangerous than, the black widow of the World Above, this Underdark spider's venom is among the deadliest naturally occurring poisons on all of Toril. This species is small enough for Matron Baenre to conceal in a ring.

GEE'AANTU

The gee'aantu are black-and-yellow spiders, similar in many ways to tarantulas. They're bred in Menzoberranzan and kept as pets by the priestesses of the Queen of the Demonweb Pits.

ORCS, GOBLINS, AND GOBLINOIDS

The savage humanoids of Faerûn are dangerous in numbers, often overrunning towns or even cities in their endless quest for spoils. Some are smarter than others, but all are violent and temperamental, driven to destruction and war by their dark gods. Still, some of them show the first traces of civilized behavior and in their own way may be developing the ability to live side-by-side with other sentient beings. Only time will tell if that will ever really be true.

ORCS

This ubiquitous race of savage humanoids has spread across Faerûn like a plague. Orcs can be found in every corner of the world but are particularly plentiful in the North. There they skulk about the Spine of the World, gathering in tribes that grow to thousands, then invariably split apart as the orcs end up fighting amongst themselves.

Orcs live by raiding their neighbors, targeting anyone or anything they feel they can beat. As often as not they underestimate their opponent's strength, so they are constantly being beaten back into their dismal, stinking caves. Still, orc hordes have been responsible for disastrous raids throughout the history of the Realms. They harbor a particular hatred of both dwarves and elves—whom orcs will attack on sight—and dwarves and elves are happy to return the favor.

Their ancient and brutish god Gruumsh demands that they march from one raid to another, sowing destruction and chaos everywhere they tread. His shamans dress in red and can incite an orc tribe to such murderous frenzy that they become like wild animals. Strength rules in orc society, which is violently male dominated. Females—orc or human, they don't care which—are traded as possessions.

BUGBEARS

Sometimes found in thrall to dark elves, and sometimes found in control of goblin tribes, bugbears are the biggest, most aggressive, and strongest of the goblinoids. Adult males stand over seven feet tall and are covered in thick, matted fur. These brutish creatures hunt the caves and ravines of mountain ranges throughout the Realms and are scattered through the upper reaches of the Underdark in small bands of fewer than fifty. Their primary concern is for treasure, which they attempt to steal from whomever they're confident they can kill.

Goblins

Goblins are scattered throughout the Realms, living in both the Underdark and in the World Above. They gather into tribes as large as four hundred but can also be found in wandering bands of less than a dozen. Solitary hobgoblins and bugbears occasionally seize control of a tribe, exerting their will over the smaller, weaker goblins by intimidation. But not all goblins are that easy to cow, many having come to understand that their rapid breeding can give them the advantage of numbers. A goblin horde on the march should not be underestimated.

Their shamans serve the vile demon god Maglubiyet, but they usually tend to make a tribe *less* civilized, since their god encourages wholesale slaughter and destruction. Even among their own tribe there's little peace, with individual goblins stealing from each other, fighting, and murdering each other with no regard for their own community—another reason why they're so easily dominated by others. Drow keep them as slaves and use them—along with kobolds—as no more than fodder.

They speak their own language—a whining, shrill sound that grates on civilized ears—and follow their savage customs when left alone, or they adapt as best they can when forced to serve. Still, it's a rare goblin slave that isn't constantly plotting the death of its master or trying to make good its escape.

Gnolls

Not quite related to goblins or orcs, gnolls appear to be seven-and-a-half-foot-tall humanoid dogs clad in whatever cast-off bits of armor and clothing they've managed to steal from their civilized victims. Though vicious and feral in temperament and appearance, gnolls have a cowardly streak that prevents them from being a greater threat than they are. It's rare that a gnoll gang will attack unless they clearly have superior numbers, but they will fight furiously when cornered.

GIANTS AND GREATER HUMANOIDS

It's difficult to know how many giants wander the frontiers of the Realms or even how many different kinds there are. These enormous creatures tend to be a solitary lot, but when they make their presence known, they are big enough and strong enough to leave an impression on even the most jaded adventurer. Some are barely more than brutes, while others are intelligent, civilized, and even learned and peaceful representatives of an ancient culture.

FROST GIANTS

Though intelligent and civilized in their own right, frost giants are hardly above the occasional raid against their neighbors and are particularly fond of taking captives. These hostages are carried back to the frost giants' freezing cavern lairs or citadels and brought before the jarl, or tribal leader. Those the jarl deems useful as slaves are kept, valuable personages are ransomed back to their families, and the rest are killed and eaten cold. Utterly inured to freezing temperatures, they love the highest mountain peaks and the coldest latitudes, often burying themselves in snow to ambush their prey.

HILL GIANTS

Hill giants, as their name would imply, inhabit the lower foothills around mountain ranges, where they make their homes in caves. Considered the least intelligent of the giants, they're also the smallest, standing a mere ten-and-half feet tall. They hunt by wandering the hills and throwing rocks and other improvised projectiles at their prey from higher ground. When forced to fight up close, they prefer clubs fashioned from tree limbs, bludgeoning away at their foes with feral abandon. They're as likely to be encountered as solitary nomads as they are to be seen in small tribes. Hill giants occasionally ally with orcs and ogres and frequently keep worgs as hunting animals and companions.

MOUNTAIN GIANTS

Mountain giants are very similar to hill giants, but four times their size, making them among the largest of the giants of Faerûn. Also, like hill giants, they're dim-witted brutes that literally stomp through the mountains, attacking villages, caravans, and travelers on a whim. So huge and strong are they that they've been known to grab a human like a doll and dash him to the ground as far as forty yards away. But a mountain giant is actually more likely just to step on you. They've never been known to gather in tribes or in any group larger than a small family unit of fewer than six individuals. Chances are, if they tried, they'd all just end up killing each other.

STONE GIANTS

The surprisingly peaceful stone giants live in clusters of small communities and cheerfully interact with others of their kind. They're the only giants known to play games, challenging each other to see who can throw a boulder the farthest or with the greatest accuracy. They're also known to be talented artists, able to shape extraordinary sculptures from rock, and they have a rhythmic music all their own. Elders of the community develop innate magical abilities that allow them to manipulate stone or change its form. Though not inherently evil, they rarely if ever seek the companionship of humans—or anyone but other stone giants—and will fight to the death to protect their communities.

OGRES

Ogres are slightly smaller than the smallest giants, standing no more than ten feet tall, and like their occasional allies the orcs, they plague humankind with bloody raids. They also live among giants and trolls, serving more powerful masters, and occasionally they take control of tribes or gangs of smaller goblinoids. It's not entirely unheard of to encounter an ogre in a human city, but the ogres' taste for human flesh generally forces civilized people to keep them at a distance.

TAERS

Taers are large, wild primates that live in sub-arctic mountains like Icewind Dale and the Spine of the World. Though hardly as intelligent as humans, they've begun to fashion crude stone weapons and will hurl stone-tipped spears at anyone who passes into their territory. They inhabit caves, mostly, living in extended family groups of a few dozen or so individuals. The language of the taers sounds like snarling and snorting to a human ear. Though reclusive, they will sometimes, but rarely, operate as mercenaries for more powerful creatures like the demon Errtu.

TROLLS

These nine-foot-tall, five hundred pound carnivorous humanoids have spread to every corner of the Realms and seem entirely indifferent to climate or geography. They tend to attack, kill, and eat everything that crosses their paths, and though they'll work with some species of giants, ogres, and other humanoids, they're most often encountered as wandering individuals. Unsubtle fighters, they attack with tooth and claw and have the ability to regenerate when wounded. Because of that, trolls are awfully hard to kill. If you cut their arms off, the claws will keep trying to fight. The only things that seem to permanently injure them are fire and acid.

CREATURES OF FAERÛN

Faerûn is a land filled with monsters. From the most densely populated cities to the most remote wildernesses, strange creatures of every size and description lurk in the shadows, hunt in starlight, or stand out under the blazing sun.

DISPLACER BEASTS

Displacer beasts are great black cats that average ten feet in length. Long tentacles, which are covered in ragged, thornlike spikes that can strip their prey of flesh, protrude from their shoulders, and their eyes shine a ghostly green. The almost humanlike cry of a displacer beast is profoundly unsettling. Displacer beasts get their name from their innate ability to shift within the fabric of dimensions, so that they appear to be some three feet or so from where they actually are. This talent makes them very difficult to fight. A displacer beast can literally ambush someone who's looking it in the eye—or thinks he's looking it in the eye. Their pelts are highly prized as cloaks, since their skin retains this power after death.

BASILISK

These enormous lizards grow to twelve or thirteen feet in length and walk on eight legs, which end in sharp claws. Their large heads are dominated by a wide, fang-lined mouth full of jagged teeth like spearheads. They have very poor eyesight and appear slow moving and lazy but are vicious and dangerous carnivores. Basilisks hide in shallow caves and crevasses from which they ambush their prey.

But the most terrifying thing about the basilisk is its petrifying gaze. Looking one in the eye results in its victim being permanently turned to stone. The entrances to their lairs are scattered with what appear to be perfectly rendered stone statues but are in fact the petrified forms of their victims.

BOG BLOKES

Three-foot-tall beings that resemble trees, bog blokes haunt the cold marshes of the North. They attack by wildly flailing their branchlike arms, furiously bludgeoning their foes. They can grab and entangle people as well, even pulling riders from their horses. Territorial and savage, bog blokes defend their marshes with deadly force.

MINOTAURS

The minotaur is a proud and territorial breed of humanoid bull. They aren't necessarily the smartest creatures but are capable of language and sometimes work metal, creating bladed weapons of their own. They're found primarily in the Underdark but have also spread to the World Above, where they have even settled in some human communities, though that's quite rare. House Baenre of Menzoberranzan maintains a number of minotaur slaves that they deploy as guards and laborers. Some were sent to attack Mithral Hall.

PEGASI

The proud, winged horses are the totem animal of the Sky Pony Tribe and are found in the wild in temperate forests all over Faerûn. They are prized as mounts, as they can carry a rider aloft with them. Intelligent and independent, a pegasus is not easily broken. Most often, when encountered as a mount, it has made the conscious decision to ally itself with someone. The elves of the Moonwood have close associations with pegasi, whom they treat as equals, not as livestock. Others beings are less enlightened and will resort to cruel methods to break these regal animals' spirits.

REMORHAZ

The dreaded polar worms are insectoid creatures that grow to lengths of forty feet or more and live in arctic climes where they hunt frost giants, polar bears, and anything else that might satisfy their appetites. They crawl around on a multitude of legs, and their bodies are long, segmented, and strong. Their backs glow red with heat that helps them melt the ice around them so they can travel unseen, ambushing their prey from below. The frost giants of the Spine of the World have taken to capturing larval remorhazes and raising them as guard monsters, though even then they're likely to turn on their masters.

TUNDRA YETIS

A tundra yeti appears to be a cross between a human and a bear, covered in thick, shaggy white fur that turns brown in the summer. They're found in Icewind Dale and other arctic regions, including the Great Glacier. It's not uncommon to come upon their wide, deep footprints in the snow but quite a bit harder to find a yeti in the flesh.

Apparently always hungry, the tundra yeti hides in tall grass in summer or under the snow in winter to pounce on its prey. They're strong enough to stop a charging horse and break its neck in the bargain. Only the mountain giant, Junger, has been known to domesticate these feral beasts, which tend to be fiercely independent and solitary. For most people the very sight of a tundra yeti is enough to paralyze them with fear—at least long enough for the yeti to finish them off.

UNICORNS

These beautiful and powerful animals are imbued with magic that makes them highly sought after as mounts and allies for the goodly races of the Realms. Unicorns will ally themselves with elves or humans when they feel that the relationship will make the world a better place. They're horses, for all intents and purposes, but with a single long, ivory horn protruding from their foreheads. Beautiful and unpredictable, they have minds and ways of their own and can be extremely dangerous when threatened. The unicorn is associated with the nature goddess Meilikki and is often used as a symbol of those who live in harmony with the natural world. A unicorn appears on coins minted in Silverymoon.

WERERATS

Wererats are wily and dangerous creatures that inhabit the sewers of larger cities throughout the Realms, from Calimport to Waterdeep. Like other lycanthropes, wererats are able to take on three different forms. The first is a rat, which appears in all ways to be a normal rodent. In their human form they retain the stench of the sewers and the twitchy, nervous behavior of their rodent form. Between rat and human, they're able to hold a transitional form, appearing as so-called "ratmen." In melee, they rely on weapons in both human and ratman form and don't tend to be too physically strong. That being the case, they avoid hand-to-hand combat, preferring to stalk their prey from the shadows, often following drunks out of sleazy taverns and dragging them down into the sewers to be devoured by their packs. Wererats gather into groups and are rarely encountered alone. These packs sometimes even take the form of thieves' guilds—wererats are notorious rogues accustomed to hiding out at the fringes of human society.

WOLVES AND WORGS

Wolves are common throughout Faerûn, especially in the temperate forests of the North. They travel in packs and hunt small animals and deer, rarely if ever attacking humans. Humans and humanoids, including orcs, occasionally take them as pets or as guard animals.

Worgs are related to the dire wolves—particularly large but otherwise normal wolves—that may have been bred intentionally to be a bit smaller but with a much keener intelligence. They're agile despite their size and weight and are valued by goblinoids as mounts. Worgs are also encountered as pets or guard animals for some species of giants, orcs, and other giantkind and goblinoids. Their fur is bristly and thick, making them hard to wound. They are able to speak a primitive language of their own and understand simple commands in Common.

If someone did intentionally breed worgs, he long ago lost control of his creation, leaving them to the wild.

BEASTS OF THE OUTER PLANES

Whatever the number of strange creatures that walk Faerûn, it's nothing compared to that of the endless expanse of the multiverse. The Abyss has more layers than have ever been counted, and all of them are full of demons, many of which have never been encountered by living mortals. The Nine Hells may be smaller, but it's teeming with terrifying devils and godlike archdevils—which makes those creatures a little more eager to travel to the Prime Material Plane in search of power and prey.

CHASME

The chasme are insectoid demons that serve as something like truant officers in the Abyss, rounding up demons that have deserted their posts and have refused to fight in the endless Blood Wars. That activity makes them rather less than popular among their demonic brethren. They also serve as messengers and servants to greater demons but still don't get much respect in the Abyss or elsewhere. Their service allows them to avoid direct conflict in the Blood Wars. Though they exist for violence and chaos, they don't seem to have a taste for warfare, preferring instead to kill weaker creatures across the planes.

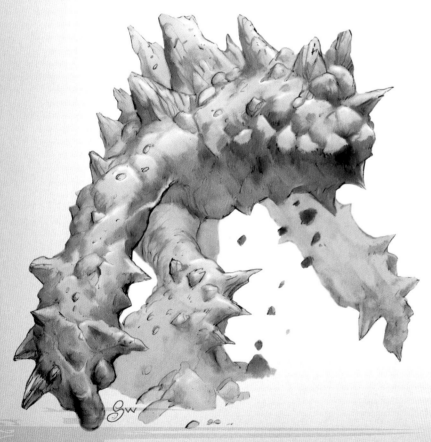

EARTH ELEMENTALS

Earth elementals are summoned from the Elemental Plane of Earth by wizards or priests in need of some muscle. They manifest on the Prime Material Plane as fifteen-foot-tall giants of living rock. Svirfneblin are particularly fond of earth elementals, and Belwar Disssengulp summons one to combat the dark elves of Menzoberranzan. Earth elementals can crush a human with ease and are incredibly difficult to destroy. It's not easy, but it is possible to dismiss them, sending them back to the plane from which they came—and where they would rather have stayed. Even the person who summons them can find them difficult to control, and elementals of all kinds have turned on and murdered their would-be masters. Any summoner's relationship with an elemental is temporary. These creatures just don't like it on the Prime Material Plane.

HELL HOUNDS

Packs of up to a dozen of these massive black dogs can be summoned from their infernal home plane and bound into service. Some have broken free of their summoners to roam Faerûn on their own, hunting dark woods or swamps or the shadowy alleyways of cities. They stand over four feet tall at the shoulder and weigh a little more than a hundred pounds. Their long, sharp fangs and equally long and sharp claws are dangerous, but hell hounds are also able to spit forth a gout of roiling fire as far as thirty feet.

SUCCUBI

A succubus appears as a beautiful young woman who seduces men of particular passion. Only when their victims are firmly in their clutches do they reveal their true forms as demonic women with batlike wings and hideous fangs. Capable of extraordinary subtlety, they can take months to properly seduce their victims, draining a little life-force with each passionate kiss. This process can be so subtle and so enjoyable for the victim that few of the men so cursed even notice anything is wrong, at least not until it's too late.

Succubi do their best to avoid direct conflict, and though they'll fight to defend themselves, they prefer the long, slow kill. They'll sometimes act in concert with other demons, but they prefer to make their own way. The succubus that tortured Wulfgar at the command of Errtu, for instance, was working off a debt to the great balor.

A DEEP DROW LEXICON

The drow are scattered across Faerûn's Underdark in dozens of isolated communities, where different dialects of a basic root language are spoken. Deep Drow, also known as Low Drow or Drowic, is the most common language used by the majority of rank-and-file dark elves. High Drow, a more complex language with a much larger alphabet, is used primarily by priestesses in their sacred rites or by other high-born drow seeking to communicate with each other without the risk that those of lower social standing—especially non-drow slaves—will understand.

Deep Drow is read right to left, with words stacked in long, single-word columns with only a scattering of punctuation. Drow writing tends to be unadorned and to the point, with little effort wasted on human conventions like exclamation points or question marks.

abban—ally
abbil—trusted comrade
akh—group
alur—superior
alurl—best
alust—in front
asanque—as you wish
avinsin—doomed
bautha—to dodge
bauth—around
belaern—wealth
belbau—to give
belbol—gift
bol—unidentified item
brorna—surprises
brorn—surprise
caballin—food
colbauth—known path
colnbluth—non-drow
dal—from
darthiir—the fey, surface elves, traitors
del—of
dobluth—outcast
doeb—out
dosstan—yourself
dosst—yours
dos—you
draa—two
drada—second
dro—life, to be alive
duk—unholy
elamshin—destiny, the will of Lolth
elend—traditional
elendar—enduring

elgg—to kill
elghinn—death
faer—magic
faerbol—magical item
faerl—magical
faern—wizard
gol—goblin
golhyrr—trick, trap
goln—goblins
harl—under, below
harl'il'cik—to kneel
haszak—illithid
haszakkin—illithids
honglath—calm, bravery
iblith—excrement
ilharessen—matrons
ilharess—matron
ilhar—to mother
ilharn—patron
ilindith—goal
insi—doom
inthigg—agreement
inth—scheme
izil—as
jabbuk—master
jal—all
jivvin—to play
jivvin quui'elghinn—to torture to death
khal'abbil—my trusted comrade
khaless—misplaced trust
kolsen'shea orbb—"to pull the legs off a spider" (idiom)
kulggen—constructed barrier
kulg—blockage
kyone—to be alert or careful

kyorlin—watching
kyorl—watch
lil—the
llarnbuss—third
llar—three
lueth—and
luth—to throw
maglust—alone
malla—honored one
mrimm—inspiration
mzild—more
natha—a
nau—no
nind—they, them, their, theirs
nindyn—those
noamuth—lost
noe—bold
noet—boldly
obsul—door or opening
ogglin—enemy
olist—stealth
oloth—darkness
orbb—spider
orthae—sacred
pera'dene—scapegoat
phalar—grave
phindar—non-intelligent monster
pholor—on, upon
phuul—are
plynn—seize
qua'laelay—disagreement
quarth—to command
quarthen—commanded
Quarvalsharess—"The Goddess" (Lolth)
quar'valsharess—other drow gods
qu'ellar—House
qu'lith—blood
qu'uente—guts
ragar—to discover
rath—back
ratha—backs
rathrae—behind
rivvil—human
rivvin—humans
sargh—skill at arms
sargtlin—drow warrior
sarn—beware
shavrak—final
sreen—danger
ssinssrigg—passion, longing

ssussun—light
streeaka—recklessness
streea—to die in the service of Lolth
taga—than
tak—executioner
talinth—to think
talthalra—meeting
thalack—war
Thalackz'hind—raid
thalra—encounter
tlu—to be
tuth—both
ul-Ilindith—destiny
uln'hyrr—liar
ultrinnan—conquering, victory, to win or prevail
ultrin—supreme
ultrine—supreme goddess (Lolth)
ulu—to
uss—one
usstan—self, I
usstil—one in my place
ust—first
valsharess—queen
veldrin—shadows
vel'uss—who
velkyn—invisible
velve—blade
waela—foolish
wael—fool
wund—among, within, into
wun—in
xal—may, might, perhaps
xund—work
xun—to work
xundus—to have worked
yath—temple
yathrin—drow priestess
yathtallar—high priestess
yorn—servant of Lolth
yorthae—chosen one
zhah—is
zhaun—to learn, to know
zhaunil—learning, wisdom
zheel—word
z'har—to ride
z'hin—to walk
z'hind—journey
z'orr—to climb
z'ress—to dominate by force of will*

SHAVRAK LIL'ZHEEL

"THE FINAL WORD"

I couldn't resist it.

They were just sitting there in a folder marked "Text Files": the complete text of all thirteen volumes of THE LEGEND OF DRIZZT. I had to add it up, and the figure came to 1,326,172.

Words.

That's a lot of words, and I can't even describe how daunting a task it was to distill those 1,326,172 words—combined with the dozens of FORGOTTEN REALMS and DUNGEONS & DRAGONS® role-playing game products that I consulted for further details—into the book you're holding in your hands. It wasn't easy, but I had a lot of help. If you've spotted any mistakes, that's all my doing. The following people made sure there weren't lots, lots more.

The best art director in the business, Matt Adelsperger, and editor extraordinaire Susan Morris held my hand through the whole thing, even when I was running hopelessly late—especially comical since I'm usually the guy who hollers at authors who are particularly late. Thanks, Matt and Susan—and sorry!

Peter Archer came to me with the idea in the first place, and Mary-Elizabeth Allen made the actual offer. Paul Bazakas, Liz Schuh, Bill Slavicsek, Jessica Blair, Jodi Medlock, Marty Durham, Hilary Ross, Cynda Callaway, Sarah Keortge, Dan Colavito, the Ryans Rosenberg and Sansaver, and all the editors, art directors, game and graphic designers, typesetters, and brand managers who came before us made it into something you could actually hold in your hands. Thanks, everyone.

The name on the overwhelming majority of those role-playing game products I mentioned is Ed Greenwood—nobody's done anything with a FORGOTTEN REALMS logo on it who doesn't owe a debt of gratitude to Ed. Thanks, Ed.

It took a massive three-inch three-ring binder to hold the hard copies of the compressed information that was gathered from the thirteen books by independent researchers we hired a very, very long time ago to help us with the ill-fated, multi-volume FORGOTTEN REALMS Encyclopedia. That encyclopedia, and the accompanying database, never saw the light of day, but I don't think a single day has gone by in a decade that I haven't referred to those reader reports for one reason or another. Those researchers are credited in the front of this book, but Julia Martin and Steven Schend aren't—and those reports would not have existed without their long hours and passionate efforts. Thanks, guys.

That art director I mentioned before is going to do his level best to credit every artist who contributed to this book, and though I guess I could have written the text without them, I can guarantee you wouldn't have enjoyed it as much. Though I appreciate every brushstroke of every artist, THE LEGEND OF DRIZZT comes alive thanks to the imagination and talent of Todd Lockwood, who just blows me away every time. Thanks, Todd.

My wife, Deanne, put up with me while I put off thinking

about this book, started the research, got paralyzed by the sheer scope of it, started the research again, started writing it, stopped, started again (lather, rinse, repeat) while whining the whole way in a sleep-deprived stupor, and she didn't leave me or anything. Thanks, Sweetie.

And then there's this big, kind of loud guy from central Massachusetts with a funny accent and a questionable haircut who had a little something to do with this as well. I can't remember his name just now, but I do remember this time we were in New York together for a book industry convention. We were having dinner in this great little Italian place just off the campus of NYU, about six or seven of us, and suddenly a man steps up behind Bob Salvatore—that's his name, Bob Salvatore—puts his hands on Bob's shoulders, and with a smile, says something like, "You're a real gentleman, thank you very much."

He was standing directly behind Bob, who didn't really look up but with a smile, said, "No problem," or something like that, and the man, who turned out to be *60 Minutes* correspondent Mike Wallace, walked away smiling.

The rest of us sat there in stunned silence for a few seconds, wondering how it's possible that Bob Salvatore and Mike Wallace were old friends—they sure seemed to know each other. Finally I had to ask, "How do you know him?"

Bob's reply: "He told me to shut up earlier, so I did."

Bob didn't even realize that the guy who had asked him to keep his voice down was Mike Wallace, but Bob had lowered his voice then convinced us all, just by being his easy-going, sincerely friendly self, that the two of them were old school chums.

That's the kind of guy Bob Salvatore is—the kind of guy who talks and laughs loudly with friends at dinner but will lower his voice if you ask him to—and because, unlike Bob and Mike Wallace, Bob and I are friends, the hard work that went into this book was worth every second.

Thanks, Bob, for the temporary loan of your legend.

—Philip Athans
January 2008

ONE DROW

HOMELAND   EXILE   SOJOURN   THE CRYSTAL SHARD   STREAMS OF SILVER   THE HALFLING'S GEM   THE LEGACY

TWO SWORDS

STARLESS NIGHT   SIEGE OF DARKNESS   PASSAGE TO DAWN   THE SILENT BLADE   THE SPINE OF THE WORLD   SEA OF SWORDS

TWENTY YEARS

THE THOUSAND ORCS   THE LONE DROW   THE TWO SWORDS   THE ORC KING   THE PIRATE KING